Screamin' Jay Hawkins' All-Time Greatest Hits

Screamin' Jay Hawkins' All-Time Greatest Hits

A NOVEL

Mark Binelli

Metropolitan Books
Henry Holt and Company
New York

Metropolitan Books
Henry Holt and Company, LLC
Publishers since 1866
175 Fifth Avenue
New York, New York 10010
www.henryholt.com

Metropolitan Books® and ⒨® are registered trademarks of
Henry Holt and Company, LLC.

Library of Congress Cataloging-in-Publication Data

Names: Binelli, Mark.
Title: Screamin' Jay Hawkins' all-time greatest hits : a novel /
    Mark Binelli.
Description: First edition. | New York : Metropolitan Books/
    Henry Holt and Company, 2016. | Includes bibliographical
    references.
Identifiers: LCCN 2015040991 (print) | LCCN 2015041777
    (ebook) | ISBN 9781627795357 (hardback) | ISBN
    9781627795364 (electronic book)
Subjects: LCSH: Hawkins, Screamin' Jay,—Fiction. |
    African American musicians—Fiction. | Biographical fiction. |
    BISAC: FICTION / Literary. | FICTION / Biographical.
Classification: LCC PS3602.I53 S34 2016 (print) | LCC
    PS3602.I53 (ebook) | DDC 813/.6—dc23
LC record available at http://lccn.loc.gov/2015040991

Our books may be purchased in bulk for promotional,
educational, or business use. Please contact your local
bookseller or the Macmillan Corporate and Premium Sales
Department at (800) 221-7945, extension 5442, or by e-mail at
MacmillanSpecialMarkets@macmillan.com.

First Edition 2016
Printed in the United States of America

10   9   8   7   6   5   4   3   2   1

For Caroline,
subject of many songs

I feel like hollering, but the town is too small.

—Big Bill Broonzy

Three of these men were at Rouen, at the time the late King Charles IX was there. The king talked to them for a long time; they were shown our ways, our splendor, the aspect of a fine city. Then someone asked them what they thought of all this and wanted to know what they had been most amazed by. They made three points; I am very annoyed with myself for forgetting the third, but I still remember two of them. In the first place they said (probably referring to the Swiss Guard) that they found it very odd that all those full-grown bearded men, strong and bearing arms in the King's entourage, should consent to obey a boy rather than choosing one of themselves as a Commander; secondly—since they have an idiom in their language which calls all men "halves" of one another—that they had noticed that there were among us men fully bloated with all sorts of comforts while their halves were begging at their doors, emaciated with poverty and hunger; they found it odd that those destitute halves should put up with such injustice and did not take the others by the throat or set fire to their houses . . .

Not at all bad, that—Ah! But they wear no breeches . . .

—Montaigne, "On the Cannibals"

Contents

Screamin' Jay Hawkins' All-Time Greatest Hits

The Funeral Procession of
Screamin' Jay Hawkins

The pallbearers entered from the right, flanking the coffin three by three. They bore the load in the old style, upon their shoulders, faces set against the task. Dragging the thing at belt's height simply would not do.

"They need to see it in you," Hawkins had explained at the first rehearsal. "Your grief over my demise."

Shouldering the coffin, to that end, was a time-honored cheat, the strain on a face only adding to the verisimilitude of the mourning. Like Stanislavsky, a shortcut to the truth of the moment.

"How do you hope to conjure the proper degree of stoical reserve," Hawkins, again, "when you dragging me around like Granny asked you to move her mattress?"

Part of the poignancy of the ritual, he told them, came from how gently the marchers performed their task. As if what they bore was not already broken.

The music preceded them. Pair of saxophones, piano. Not exactly funereal. The pianist working a languid cathouse roll, locked in vaudevillian back-forth with the rude, thrusting bursts of horn. Hawkins had instructed the pallbearers not to attempt to march in step with the tune's waltz tempo, an action which would have lent an awkward, herky-jerk rhythm to their task.

Nonetheless, the casket dipped with every fifth step or so, a skiff in a mild current.

"Slow down," Hawkins whispered, from inside. "You Irish or something? Can't wait to bury me, get right to the liquor?"

Underbreath, the pallbearers composed mock eulogies.

Precious in the sight of the Lord is the death of His saints . . .
But we're here to talk about Jalacy Hawkins.

Hawkins kept missing the punch lines. Only caught the muffled laughter, afterward.

Loving. Obedient. Generous.
Are not words you should expect to hear tonight.
He lived as he died.
Unnecessarily.
Tragically.
Facedown in a filthy water closet.

They sported matching suits, white gloves, stepped with swaying precision. It was the measured gait of a drunk attempting a dignified exit, here placed in the service of ceremony, given a sacramental pace. Like the methodical unfurling of the royal carpet, a priest lifting wafer to lips.

Blessed are they that mourn, for they shall be comforted.
Shoulders quaking alongside the titters.

If considered from the perspective of realism, the suits, to be honest, played as too smart for the occasion, it generally being considered bad form to upstage bride or corpse.

Hawkins, who had been staring at the underside of the lid, closed his eyes and tried to enjoy the feeling of floating. But that only reminded him of how much he disliked the ocean. Really, any body of water deep enough to prevent him from touching bottom.

The first rehearsal, held one week earlier, had been a cappella. Everyone agreed this created a morbid air.

CHAPTER ONE

Screamin' Jay Hawkins' All-Time Greatest Hit

The origin story typically goes something like this: On September 12, 1956, a rhythm-and-blues aspirant named Jalacy Hawkins, twenty-seven years old, native of Cleveland, entered a New York recording studio to cut a handful of sides for Okeh Records, a subsidiary of the Columbia label. One of the songs Hawkins brought to the session, an original he'd penned himself, followed a heartbroken protagonist who, in a fit of desperation, turns to black magic to beguile the strayed object of his affection.

He'd actually recorded another version of "I Put a Spell on You" months earlier. It's difficult to imagine, considering the sturdiness of Hawkins' baritone, but at that time, he crooned the number entirely straight. His model was Johnny Ace, the Memphis preacher's son with the impossibly tender voice—specifically, the hit single "Pledging My Love," a favorite of Hawkins', with its syrupy arrangement, heavy on the tinkling vibes, Johnny purring the lyrics like a lullaby.

Forrrrever my darrrrling...

That one.

"I Put a Spell on You" was a sweet ballad when I wrote it.

Arnold Maxin, the Columbia A&R man meant to supervise the session, wasn't interested in ballads, though. Rock and roll, that mongrel genre, with its raw appeals to youth, had become the sound of the moment. Hawkins and the session musicians, to Maxin, sounded hopelessly stiff by comparison. In frustration, he ordered up a case of cheap wine: Swiss Colony, an Italian muscatel.

We all got blind drunk.

The singer awoke the following afternoon, worked over by a brute of a hangover, the rest of the night lost in the fog of war. Nearly two weeks later, when Maxin presented him with a newly pressed 78 recording of "I Put a Spell on You," Hawkins hardly recognized his song. Its melody had been sliced apart and overtaken by a shuffling somnambulist's rhythm, the vocal track similarly debased by a series of "drunken screams and groans and yells" (Hawkins' words). His sweet ballad, ensorcelled, now walked like a zombie, the arms of his lovelorn hero, thus embodied, no longer outthrust to embrace, but to strangle.

And that is how I became Screamin' Jay Hawkins.

Ten days later, he had to learn the song.

It's a great story, one that Hawkins told again and again. His masterpiece, born in the missing hours of a bacchanal! The tale has an archetypal purity: magic elixirs granting dark wishes to the imbiber, the bitter taste only hinting at the hidden price to come; a hidden Hyde, coaxed to the surface by chemistry and hubris.

The anecdote has been dutifully reprinted in liner notes, profiles, and capsule biographies. The only problem is, it's almost certainly untrue. Like many of the plot strands Hawkins affixed to the narrative of his own life—that he'd been adopted and raised by a tribe of Blackfoot Indians, that he'd studied opera at a Cleveland conservatory, that he had lied about his age at fourteen in order to join the army during the Second World War, that he'd been a middleweight boxing champion in Alaska, that he had fathered seventy-five illegitimate children—the notion of a liquid muse wildly conjuring "I Put a Spell on You" is most useful as evidence of the singer's penchant for self-mythologizing.

The reality, on the other hand, was likely far more quotidian. It turns out Hawkins loved, and unabashedly modeled his persona after, blues shouters like Wynonie Harris and and the mad swing vocalist Slim Gaillard. On his very first recorded song, a Tiny Grimes number called "Why Did You Waste My Time?" cut four years before "I Put a Spell on You," Hawkins begins to openly sob around the two-minute mark. The incipient screaming on "No Hug No Kiss," recorded at the same session, is more of a humid, viscera-soaked wail, here triggered when a voice, possibly Grimes', pleads, "Take it easy, man. You don't want her to be back. Everything gonna be alright!"

Listen to either of these tracks and there's no denying "I Put a Spell on You" rests comfortably along the same hysterical continuum. Which is not to argue against the song's eccentric, sui generis brilliance. A perfect mitteleisenhower artifact from rock and roll's unruly pubescence, "Spell" has dated atypically well. One attempts to reverse engineer the alchemy at work and comes up short. At heart, of course, the song is a joke, the bawdiness of a waltz as channeled by a piano player in a saloon, a horn section frothing itself to a frenzy, Hawkins' loopy and parodic baritone, his winking delivery at once ironizing the material and including himself in the gag. But somehow, after all these years, "Spell" still retains a lingeringly sinister air.

Consider the lyrics, often overlooked—in particular, the excellent twist that comes about when Hawkins reveals the final three words of the title phrase: *Because you're mine.*

Isolated like so, it's a Cole Porter fragment, just about. But in context, you have to wonder, why bother with all of this hoodoo jive if she *already* belongs to you, man? *I've placed you under a spell because I possess you*: granted, there's a perverse, near-tautological elegance to the claim. Though it also sounds like a threat. Later in the number, Hawkins menacingly flips the question of ownership, *because you're mine* metamorphosing into

> I don't *care* if you want me
> I'm *yours* right now

Emphasis the singer's. Doesn't sound like a gift.

Aside from "I Put a Spell on You," Hawkins' legacy rests primarily upon his outrageous live show. Pallbearers hauled him onstage in a coffin. (Alan Freed's idea. Hawkins always hated climbing into that box. His heavy drinking began, he said, as a means of coping with his nightly entombments.) He wore a cape, clamped a bone to his nose, and carried a staff topped with a human skull. The skull's name was Henry.

It's difficult to overstate the sheer perversity of the choice, especially considering the historical tendency among music fans (i.e., white music fans) to exoticize African American artists, Robert Johnson's devil-hocked soul only the most prominent example of a racialized infatuation with black masculinity, carnality, appetite, transgression—in a word, *authenticity*—that's permanently distorted the ways in which we all think about, and listen to, music, and which demands a requisite level of "realness" from so many of our performers, who, never mind the songs, must also be junkies, killers, out-laws, colorfully touched, fiending on something, primitives whose compositions aren't written so much as discharged, ideally from a suppurating wound. This is not the history of black music in America, but of its commodification, from which Screamin' Jay Hawkins, this most deliberately inau-thentic of performers, stands apart.

The early notoriety of "I Put a Spell on You" would mold his stage persona forever, prompting him to embrace, for the remainder of his career, cartoonish witch doctor imagery straight out of Hollywood B-pictures. Surely in part for that reason, he never achieved anything like that success again. Today's average music listener has more likely heard one of the famous cover versions of "I Put a Spell on You" (Nina Simone's overproduced, melodramatic dirge, Creedence Clear-water Revival's bar-band atrocity) than Hawkins' original. The song did periodically resurface on enough occasions (most notably, in the 1984 Jim Jarmusch film *Stranger Than Para-dise*) to grant the singer a certain cult status in the final years of his life. To Hawkins, most likely, the embrace felt little and belated. Back in the early sixties, his career had found-ered so spectacularly he'd been forced to take a gig as the musical act at a Honolulu strip club.

If there's something unsettling about a black American so gleefully embodying such crude racial caricature—the NAACP would call Hawkins out, denouncing his act along-side square parents and skittish radio programmers—there's also a postmodern tweaking of (white) audience expectation going on. Ditto the "Screamin'" part of the act, for Hawkins surely understood, as Albert Murray writes in the brilliant *Stomping the Blues*, the ways in which "references to singing the blues have come to suggest crying over misfortune . . . a species of direct emotional expression in the raw, the natural outpouring of personal anxiety and anguish," when in fact artists announcing themselves as blues musicians "do not mean they are about to display their own raw emotion. They are not really going to be crying, grieving, groaning, moaning, or shouting and screaming."

Such a reading "ignores what a blues performance so obviously is," Murray continues. "It is precisely an artful contrivance."

CHAPTER TWO

Born and Abandoned

The mother had come west to bear the child. It was July 1929. West to Cleveland, three months before the crash.

Wilson, the lay handyman at St. Jude's, an asylum for destitute and abandoned children, discovered the boy in his wheelbarrow, swaddled in quilting. Minutes later, he burst into the breakfast assembly, announcing with an idiot's grin, "Some fool has left a lump of coal on our doorstep, Father Nowicki!"

In the note, the mother hinted at a row with her family, subsequent disowning. For her loose ways, one would assume.

Handsome enough child, for all that. She had named him Jalacy, after a neighborhood juice cart. The owner had been an Arabian fellow.

"Do they think," Wilson, unveiling the pipsqueak, trying again to coax a smile from the priest, "we light our furnace in the summertime?"

St. Jude's also took in adults (feebleminded or crippled), and Sister Frederick, the senior nun on the hospital staff, generally avoided working with the youngsters. But she would always remember the boy, or claim to.

"Had you seen the child back then," she would insist, "you, too, would appreciate the irony. Scream? Ho."

Not a peep. He stared at you, like a little man. Like a skeptic.

One evening in the nursery, long after the dousing of the lamps, the regular girl having taken ill, Sister Frederick performed the nightly rounds. She found all of the children asleep and at peace, except for the boy. *That* one lay on his back, with his eyes wide open, as if awaiting the tit. But so still, she thought the worst, right off, and must have loosed a gasp. At the sound, he swiveled his head in her direction and fixed her with a cold glower. Such a serious expression on that face!

"What's wrong with you, now?" she whispered. "It's dark outside. You must rest. Don't you like to rest?"

He gazed directly into her eyes, blinking calmly.

"Sleepy, sleepy," she whispered, hoping to suggest, and closing her own eyes, to demonstrate. But she could still feel that unnatural gaze burning her skin. Sure enough, when she peeked again, he just lay there, aloof as a senator.

"Cuckoo!" she began to whisper. She'd become desperate, by this point, to force a smile out of the boy. "Cuckoo! Cuckoo!"

Nothing. Suddenly, she felt embarrassed. As if she were playing the clown in the presence of a peer.

Can you imagine? Reddened by that little plum pit?

"Are you familiar with his music, Sister?" a visitor once wondered, years later.

Oh, yes: she loved nothing better than a sock hop!

She was not familiar with his music.

Eyes that judged, and not a sound.

Jalacy liked to tell people he'd been raised by a tribe of Blackfoot Indians, an impossibly romantic notion for an orphan—adoption by tribe!—though it was a young couple who had contacted Father Nowicki, the director of St. Jude's, concerning the possibility of taking in a child.

Peering nervously into the visiting room the afternoon after the phone call, the priest and his secretary, Brother Karl, spotted a man in a feathered headdress, a tan leather vest, and vivid facial "war paint."

"Purely decorative, one should hope," Father Nowicki murmured.

"He seems very . . . stoic," whispered Brother Karl.

"A long-suffering people," Father Nowicki replied. "*That*, none can deny."

This particular Indian turned out to be an adult inmate named Herman Shapiro, deranged at Verdun after a mustard gas attack. The actual Blackfeet had been sitting patiently on a chair meant for one, the prospective father perched on an overstuffed arm. The man wore a tight herringbone suit and held his hat in his lap; his wife, a muted knee-length jersey dress enlivened with a yellow carnation.

Father Nowicki had decided to offer the couple the colored child. If they were in any way disappointed, they did not reveal it.

"So healthy!" the man exclaimed as his wife silently cradled Jalacy. Without looking at Father Nowicki, he continued, "We already have two daughters of our own. But we just wanted a boy. Our girls need a stinker. Someone to pull their braids, expose them to rude noises."

"I can't have any more children," the wife explained brusquely.

At this moment, the boy, tugging on a stuffed ragamuffin the wife had produced from her purse, suddenly tossed the doll to the ground and began to wriggle and fuss.

The husband lifted Jalacy from his wife's arms and, clutching the child under the armpits, used his thumbs to pat out a light percussion on either breastbone. At the same time, as if dusting off an old bedtime song, he launched into a recent popular tune by Millicent Morrow, his attempt at a feminine trill at once spoofing and oddly sincere.

> Don't cry, boy,
> Though it's true I'm a-leavin'
> (And yet . . . !)
> Too much joy
> Might wind up deceivin'
> (You think . . . ?)
>
> Without dull
> Who needs dancin'?
> Without rent
> We'd all live in mansions
> (But would they still be mansions?)
> Well I don't think so
> But I'm no philosopher
> So what the (hey!) do I know?
>
> Just one thing
> Now this part is certain
> Take a bit of comfort

That after this hurtin'
The next girl you meet
Will seem awful sweet
I'm easy to beat
Won't that be a treat?
(I'm not sure if . . .)
Well I am!
Au revoir, kiddo!
Sayonara!
Ciao!
Bye-eye-eye-eye-eye . . .

The couple had met and married on a Montana reservation, eventually moving to Cleveland to find work; after a string of menial jobs, the husband became a chief mixer at Henry Sherwin's paint factory. They settled in the Central Avenue district, populated, primarily, by blacks and Jewish and Italian immigrants. Jalacy's references to his new family as a "tribe" were an embellishment, of course. Though it was true that certain of the neighbors privately referred to the Indians as such.

Piano lessons. Catch. Mother's cooking. Tag. Sister-fights. Foot races. A bicycle. Saturday matinees. School, mostly dull.

Fishing from the pier, using lumps of cheese gummed to a hook.

The high dive. That awful climb. Other kids clowning, pretending they'd been convicted of treason on the high seas and forced to walk the plank.

Jalacy could never take the high dive lightly.

On Tuesdays, the dreaded "boiled dinner." (Chicken or brisket, with carrots, potatoes.) Jalacy's favorite meal: city chicken, actually cubed pork scraps on a stick, breaded and then baked in the oven.

Jacks. Box fort. The alley behind Kelvin's garage, narrow enough to feel like a tunnel.

Holding a girl's fingers during a movie. Clustered sticks.

Hurling lit matches at each other in the field behind the Fords'.

White Zombie, starring Bela Lugosi. Also, *The Magic Island*, chronicling true-life encounters with the mystical in Haiti. One of his favorite books as a boy. After, Jalacy began walking stiff-armed, pretending at being the risen dead. He liked this idea better than heaven.

He also played at blind once. Marched into a door.

Squirrel hunting with his Indian grandfather in the tiny yard behind the house on Amos. The yard was indistinguishable from any other on the block, an entire alley's worth of them set behind a string of row houses. It had just enough room for a vegetable garden, which attracted the squirrels.

Jalacy and his grandfather propped open the double doors of his father's toolshed to form a crude partial blind. For seats, they upturned a pair of buckets and set them between the doors. It was a crisp December morning, which gave the summery odors released from the shed—a manure-encrusted shovel propped in the corner, next to the oily push-mower, dried grass forming barnacles on its blades—an almost gaseous quality. Jalacy's grandfather settled creakily atop one of the buckets and stared hard at the garden. Since he'd left the hospital, his naturally ruddy complexion had returned, and he looked almost puffy at times. Jalacy's mother told the children not to get their hopes up, that the doctor had told her it was fluids making him swell from his organs failing.

The previous summer, the grandfather had planted a patch of radicchio, a hearty lettuce favored by their Italian neighbor, alongside the perennial corn, squash, okra, zucchini, turnips. If covered with sheets of plastic, radicchio, he had been assured, could survive the winter. This morning, reflected through the sheeting and surrounded by snow, the hazy green square looked like vegetation at the bottom of a frozen pond.

Jalacy was the one to spot the squirrel, plump and gray, perched on a fence post. The grandfather lifted his gun, an ancient .22 rifle, in a smooth, swift motion and clicked off the safety latch.

"There he is!" the boy whispered. A moment earlier, he could not have cared less about the squirrel hunt. But now, with the thrill of the sighting, he'd become eager to see something die.

"Not while it's on the fence," the grandfather said.

The squirrel dived to the ground and began to scurry across the yard. At the edge of the garden, it paused in a final, twitchy pose. The boy heard the sharp crack of the rifle; across the yard, the squirrel performed a comical backflip. It looked as if it had been slapped.

Jalacy raced over to the kill, his legs tingling from the crouch. Up close, though, he felt a twinge of disappointment. The squirrel looked puny, like something that might fall out of the pocket of someone's coat.

He made no move to touch it.

Finally, his grandfather arrived. He moved very slowly.

"What's wrong?" he asked. "Would you like me to shoot him again? That make you feel safer?"

The boy shook his head no.

"Well, pick him up, then."

Jalacy hesitated, then reached down and grabbed the squirrel. It made no attempt to wriggle or bite. It was truly dead.

The grandfather snatched it out of his hand.

"Not poor-sized," he said. "First lesson is, always aim for the head. That way, you won't ruin the meat."

He insisted the boy remove his glove and feel the bullet hole, nearly invisible in the crook of the squirrel's walnut skull. The bullets of the .22 rifle were approximately the size of the tip of a pencil. A small amount of blood seeped from the squirrel's mouth. Otherwise, the kill had been quite neat.

The grandfather made his hand into a scale and bobbled the carcass. "Don't need to throw him back, huh?" he said, chuckling. For a moment, he seemed unsteady on his feet.

They took the squirrel into the cellar. The grandfather cleared a space on his workbench.

"Still warm is best," he said. "Wait too long and you're plucking chicken."

Jalacy had never plucked a chicken, but he nodded as if he understood.

"Still warm," the grandfather continued, "the skin comes right off."

As he spoke, the grandfather rummaged for a heavy pair of butcher's shears from a wooden toolbox. Then he unceremoniously snipped off the squirrel's head, tail, and feet. The detached parts fell into a neat pile. They looked like pieces to a disturbing board game. Delimbed and headless, the squirrel's torso had become a furry sausage. Quick as a surgeon, the grandfather swapped the shears for a boning knife and cut a horizontal slit into the center of the squirrel's back, only slightly wider than a button notch in an overcoat. Forcing the slit apart with his fingers, he slowly worked the meat loose. It was a deep red, the color of wine. The fur came off inside-out, like a tight-fitting glove. The grandfather used his fingers to yank off the saclike guts and the thin blade of the knife to scrape the rest of the meat clean of fat.

When he'd finished, what remained looked so much smaller than even the squirrel had. It seemed, suddenly, such a pathetic thing, what they had done.

* * *

Summers, sleeping on the porch.

Slingshots. Marbles. Stomping across his sisters' hopscotch squares. Hurling his chest through their jumping rope, as if he were breaking a finish line.

Saturday matinees. *Captains Courageous. Dick Tracy. Elephant Boy. Heidi. The Dawn Patrol. Son of Frankenstein. Billy the Kid Returns.*

A book report in the first grade on his favorite animal, the cheetah, focusing largely upon its speed.

Snowmen. Igloos. Sledding on garbage can lids.

Songs heard on the radio his mother rarely switched off. "December Valentine." "Douai (Have a Chance in France?)." "Dusk in Den Helder." "Snowflakes Never Last." "The Night They Called the Game for Rain." "Nicht So Gut." "Sentimental So-and-So." "Skid Rose." "Cora, Incommoded."

His father taught him how to ride a bike by holding on to the seat and jogging alongside. Jalacy had been furiously pedaling for some distance before he glanced to his right and realized the old man had secretly let go. Panicking, he immediately lost his balance and crashed to the ground.

His father shouting, "It's all in your head!"

Other films Jalacy would later recall as seminal influences he'd never actually seen as a boy. His memories of these movies came, primarily, from a single book, one of his favorites back then, *A Pictorial History of Horror Movies*, which, as its title suggests, comprised mostly photographs. Specifically, motion picture stills taken from the silent-film era up through the present day: Karloff, Lugosi, Lon Chaney Jr.

Jalacy couldn't remember much about the text itself, other than the book's frontispiece of classic quotations, perhaps a dozen, presented like fragments of poetry or bizarre aphorisms, many of which he would be able to recite by heart until the day he died.

> Mad? I, who have solved the secret of life, you call me mad?
> —Dr. Otto von Niemann (Lionel Atwill),
> *The Vampire Bat*, 1933

> I meddled in things that man must leave alone!
> —Jack Griffin (Claude Rains), *The Invisible Man*, 1933

> To die! To be really dead! That must be glorious!
> —Count Dracula (Bela Lugosi), *Dracula*, 1931

And Jalacy's personal favorite:

> Feast your eyes, gloat your soul, on my accursed ugliness!
> —the Phantom (Lon Chaney),
> *The Phantom of the Opera*, 1925

The pictures themselves, he mostly took in without context—without "plot" or "suspense." Which actually made them scarier, on a certain level.

Flipping ahead, there was the Phantom, arms crossed, teeth rotted, eyes encircled with black, nose tragically upturned, double chin, thin hair greasily combed over a head that's more skull, staring intently at the beautiful girl who hasn't noticed.

A screaming man (a former concert pianist) in a hospital bed recovering from a car accident, holding up a pair of enormous casts. Not yet knowing that onto his bleeding stumps have been grafted *the hands of a killer*!

Brains floating in aquariums and exposed white necks and wolfish underbites.

Jutting foreheads, faces splashed with acid, Caligari's sleepwalker standing at attention.

A decapitated head on a serving tray, startling the maid.

His first taste of the death fear came one night while saying his prayers, when he reached the "forever and ever" part of the Our Father. He took a moment to consider infinity. Even with God and his family, in heaven, still . . . *infinity*?

He began to cry.

Then, on his seventh birthday, he fell into a deep depression, at once acutely aware of the fact that he was getting older; it made him sad, this conscious realization of the passage of time.

The few adults he told were largely unsympathetic.

* * *

Following the Negro League on the radio. The Cleveland Buckeyes, the home team, of course. Though Jalacy secretly preferred the Ethiopian Clowns, the comic barnstorming club out of Miami. The radio announcer's descriptions of the antics of Richard "King Tut" King, who, prior to the arrival of the dwarf Spec Bebop, reigned as the Clowns' most lovable slapsticker. The way the announcer's voice would rise, with mock incredulity, feigned shock, intentionally melodramatic outrage, at every one of Tut's bobbled catches, catastrophic ump-collisions, mimed overswings. "And there goes his *bat* . . . right into the stands! Ladies and gentlemen, never in my life . . . Duck, Reverend, duck!"

That's the way Jalacy remembered it. In fact, Negro League games were rarely, if ever, broadcast on the radio.

Jalacy was eight years old the first time he heard live music outside of church. This happened at the Great Lakes Exposition of 1937, Cleveland's version of a World's Fair. His best friend Gilbert Erdman had invited him. The theme of the expo, "The Romance of Iron and Steel," was meant to reflect local industrial concerns (still extant, if not exactly thriving), and so Jalacy and Gilbert (along with Gib's three younger brothers) found themselves excitedly strapping lanterns to their foreheads and racing through the plaster-of-Paris tunnels of mocked-up mines; later, a waxwork Henry Bessemer welcomed them at the entrance of an unlit blast furnace, sample lumps of pig iron piled beside him. Gib, a car buff, especially enjoyed the display of classic models from Cleveland's now-defunct automotive industry—electric Bakers, luxury Peerlesses, steam-powered Whites—along with a futuristic, conceptual Dream Bus roughly the size of a backwoods tabernacle.

Sixteen months earlier, Gilbert's father had responded to an advertisement in the *Plain Dealer* offering opportunity for the area's numerous jobless to participate in a mass-scale "lakefront beautification project." With the country at large, and the beleaguered "Sixth City" in particular, still in the throes of the Great Depression, the expo had been conceived as a sort of public works project, a means of boosting the Cleveland economy by, in essence, erecting a miniature (and, not incidentally, gleaming and idealized) second metropolis in the very heart of the ailing original. The site chosen, on the shores of Lake Erie, had been, only six months earlier, a garbage dump, the rotting dockyards more or less abandoned following the stock market crash, as Cleveland's viability as a hub of lake commerce grew increasingly untenable. Mr. Erdman had lost his job at the paint factory several months earlier, and he became one of the bodies deployed to haul off the trash, posthaste.

As they toured the fairgrounds, Mr. Erdman described his first day on the job. The dump had sprawled over 150 acres, making it more of a discrete landscape, the ragged peaks suggesting geology. Work began in March, and everything remained frozen, the tin cans, broken saw blades, bed springs, and other metallic refuse not yet gone to rust, all glittering in the cloudless afternoon sunlight, seeming in fact to quiver and flow, like watery veins, some complex irrigation system feeding the piles. Some of the men had been handed picks and shovels, but Mr. Erdman had been chosen to operate one of the mechanized earth movers, a Cat Sixty, a big crawler with bull grader blades attached to the front. "They had to stop using wagons for the hauling off," he told the boys. The horses had bucked at the stench. Mr. Erdman and the other workers bound the lower halves of their faces with scarves, handkerchiefs, old rags, any method of gag against the smell. Vaseline under the nose also helped. Lunch, off-site, bandannas tugged down, everyone sported a shiny mustache.

They lingered at various traditional midway distractions. Jalacy witnessed an eight-foot python swallowing a live goat; a Portuguese fisherman posing beside a ninety-pound sturgeon; John Dillinger Sr., the elderly sire of the late gangster, displaying baby pictures and varied personal effects of his wayward son, in between proselytizing in favor of the death penalty; actors on a riser performing a loud, abbreviated version of the recent Broadway hit *The Drunkard*; obese ballerinas; "The Death Coach of President Abraham Lincoln!"; embryos ranging in age from three days to eight months, arranged sequentially in jars of corresponding sizes, in an exhibit titled "The Bouquet of Life"; and a pair of boxing cats. The latter were held upright with marionette strings, with miniature gloves affixed to their front paws—to disappointing effect, despite the promise of such a spectacle.

As for music, the choices ranged from a primitive Baptist choir shape-singing on the hour in front of the Winterland Fountain to the one-man band raucously supporting the terrifying pas de chat of the aforementioned obese ballerinas. But Jalacy only made mention, later in life, of the Aquacade, a floating stage designed especially for the exposition by Billy Rose, the famed show business impresario, who had been charged with devising an unforgettable centerpiece for the park and thus seized upon the most spectacular resource at hand, the lake itself.

As Jalacy and the Erdmans crowded into the grandstand, a fanfare sounded across the water. Soon, the music was interrupted by a loud explosion, also coming from the direction of the stage, which floated approximately sixty feet from the shore, and with the explosion rose a curtain—a curtain of water, projected from jets sunk in front of the stage. Jalacy clutched his slice of bleacher and leaned forward, a rapt human gargoyle, his short legs clamping the underside of the bench to prevent an unintentional somersault.

The stage disappeared behind the water-wall, soaring upwards of forty feet. The crowd whooped and pounded the bleachers. Eventually, as the jets reduced their force, lowering the curtain, a wondrous, teeming set was revealed. Elaborately costumed bathing beauties arranged themselves like an unfurled banner across the sand of an artificial beach. A pair of high dives, off to either side, faced the audience. Actual banners hung their lengths, covering the ladders. The left read: ACT ONE. The right: CALIFORNIA. A painted backdrop depicted the Hollywood Hills, the city's famous sign, naturally, included.

At this point, the swimsuit-clad chorus girls parted to reveal the stars of the show, Johnny Weissmuller and Eleanor Holm Jarrett, the champion Olympic swimmers, who strolled to the front of the stage with an unhurried noblesse befitting of their stature.

"Look, kiddo, it's Tarzan!" Mrs. Erdman whispered to Gilbert.

Jalacy's mother had taken him to see Weissmuller's second Tarzan picture, *Tarzan and His Mate*, three years earlier. He'd been too young to appreciate Maureen O'Sullivan's skimpy costume, and in fact, only two moments from the film remained fixed in his memory: Weissmuller straddling a rhinoceros and riding it like a steed through the jungle and another scene in which a pair of African natives tumble from a tree and wind up eaten by lions. Both set pieces had prompted cheers from the audience.

"Hello, Cleveland!" Weissmuller, the big Transylvanian, cried into a microphone.

Holm merely smiled and waved. She had been thrown off the Olympic team one year earlier, after drinking herself unconscious while on a cruise ship en route to Germany for the Berlin Games. Champagne, reportedly. At the time, she'd professed not to understand the fuss, telling a reporter, "I'm twenty-two, white and free."

The show proceeded in short order, moving rapidly through four acts. After California, there was Coney Island, Florida, and, inevitably, Lake Erie. The water curtain rose with every set change; successive backdrops depicted Luna Park and a row of pastel-colored Miami Beach hotels built in the Art Deco style, before disappearing entirely for the final act to reveal a hazy, distant view of the shores of Ontario. When not swimming, Weissmuller and Holm made for genial emcees. The water ballerinas, meanwhile, had dived into the murky lake, where they proceeded to form pleasing, intricate shapes, both representational and abstract, though more than the shapes themselves, it was the fluidity of the shifting that conjured delight, as when gazing through a prism.

There were also South American high divers, swimming clowns, miniature replicas of famous battleships, and a donkey in a life vest. The miniature battleships fired off a salute to the antifascists. The clowns dog-paddled in contrapuntal circles, often colliding, and forever laughing at one another's running makeup and flattened side-curls, the latter made Hebraic by the soaking, the makeup coloring their wakes, leaving a pinkish surface scum that trailed them like long, dirty ribbons.

Jalacy's eyes remained fixed upon the house band, the Bob Crosby Orchestra, a twelve-piece ensemble specializing in the Dixieland jazz made popular in New Orleans twenty years earlier. By 1936, Crosby's music would have been considered old-fashioned by fans of the more modern big-band sounds of Duke Ellington and Benny Goodman. But for Jalacy, who had no concept of such distinctions, hearing a live orchestra proved a thrill. All of the diving and swimming and clowning, the cheers of Gib's parents and brothers and of the surrounding audience—he had never been in the midst of so many people before—even Billy Rose's patriotic speech at the climax of the show, none of this gripped Jalacy from the inside, as the music had, and pulled forth such an unfamiliar ache. Throughout the din, his gaze bored with a telescopic intensity upon the band alone. The Erdmans assumed he was captivated by the aquatic stunts.

After the show, Crosby and his players remained on the bandstand, while the set was cleared to make room for a dance floor.

"Look, Mother, the stage . . . it's moving!" one of Gib's younger brothers cried.

Sure enough, the entire stage had begun to shift forward, slow as a barge. The grind of hidden underwater conveyors was audible from the bleachers. After a few minutes, the stage had bumped flush with a dock at the base of the grandstand, and couples scrambled onto the bobbing parquet, by now thoroughly dried of any traces of water so as to prevent any tumbles. Children were not allowed onto the dance floor, but the Erdman parents could not resist taking a few spins while the boys watched from their seats.

Bob Crosby, Bing's blandly handsome younger brother, hired to lead the band because of his name rather than for any innate musical talent, stood in the center of the bandstand, the orchestra wrapped behind him in a U-shaped phalanx. He made for a likable enough face, conducting the proceedings with his right hand, which he held palm-down, his arm pivoting as rapidly as a man bouncing a ball, all the while loosely keeping time with the music. To Crosby's left,

Gil Rodin, the tenor sax player who in reality led the band, shuffled his feet in his patented "granny dance," never once rising from his chair, his saxophone bobbing up and down between his legs like a giant beak. Crosby would occasionally turn to Rodin and grin, the motion of his right hand slowing as if to say, "Easy, *easy,* boy," in the manner of someone petting a horse. Dancing couples twirled past Crosby in his crowded cove. One of the trumpet players stood on a chair and dramatically worked his horn with a plunger.

Oddly, though, the song Jalacy fixated upon featured only two members of the orchestra, drummer Ray Bauduc and bassist Bob Haggart. It was one of the simplest in the group's repertoire, a novelty whistling tune called "Big Noise from Winnetka." Bauduc and Haggart had written the song on the fly, improvising it during an encore at a VFW dance in Winnetka, Illinois.

"*Winnetka,*" Crosby informed the crowd in his introduction, "is Indian for 'beautiful land.'"

The song was undeniably catchy, and perhaps Jalacy, his taste still immature, responded to the instant gratification of its easy charms, beginning with Bauduc's tiptoed opening drumroll, closely followed by Haggart climbing up and down the stairs on his big double bass. Hag also provided the melody, breaking into a reedy, workmanlike whistle. His method involved assuming an overbite and pushing air through his bucked teeth, an old jobbers' trick, effective if visually unpleasant. You could almost hear his tongue getting in the way. And there was Ray B., hunched over his kit, head ducked as if he'd thrown out his back at the downbeat of a shrug, turning his attentions, eventually, to a single cymbal, doing detail work on it, a painter fussing over his palette. Hag kept the neck of his bass hugged to his shoulder. His whistle, as high and fluttering as a marcher's fife, undergirded by the steady rumble of his bass and Bauduc's drums, made Jalacy think of a butterfly crossing a battlefield. As the song approached its climax, the pair leaned in close. Hag tilted his bass's neck until it practically touched Bauduc's hair, allowing Bauduc to reach over and strum the bassline with one of his sticks, Haggart handling the fingering, one-handed, up top.

The kind of whistle you'd use on a girl.

It was like nothing else Jalacy had ever seen or heard before, and he hoped it never stopped.

"Moon-Eyed and Mackereled." "Maestro, Your Baton." "Rigmarole." "Bippity Bop." "What's So Wonderful (About His Girl)?." "Ten Minutes Past Yesterday." "Mute Over You." "Sucker Bet." "Spec Bebop's Zulu Jive."

Back then, no such thing as trick-or-treating. On Halloween, they would eat dinner in silence. Jalacy's father, referring to the meal as a "dumb feast," promised if they remained quiet enough, a ghost might join them at the table. Jalacy was never quite sure if his father actually believed such a benevolent haunting could occur or if the story had been invented to frighten and amuse them. In either case, Jalacy sincerely tried to listen for spooks. Not that you'd be able to hear one, unless it deliberately chose to knock over a vase or moan faintly in your ear.

As an extrasensory cue, he tried to recall the voices of the few people he'd known who had died. He'd been too young when his grandmother passed to allow for a proper conjuring of her speech, leaving him with Mr. Gerhardt, the butcher, who used to present Jalacy, if he happened to accompany his mother on her shopping rounds, with a cold sausage for a treat. Mr. Gerhardt had been struck and killed by a streetcar on the way to the shop one morning. Children in the neighborhood said his legs had been severed, and that he'd bled to death in the street, cursing God and howling like a dog. Jalacy didn't know about that. Mr. Gerhardt's voice, though, had been full of sawdust, rising and falling in an easily imitable manner.

During the dumb feast, as he attempted to chew with as much delicacy and quiet self-control as he could manage, Jalacy would picture Mr. Gerhardt behind his counter in his bloody butcher's apron. He thought perhaps his mother made her knife squeak against her plate in noisier fashion than required, in passive protest of an annual ritual she found inane. He could hear his eldest sister swallowing, and the creak of a chair, as someone shifted in their seat. He stared at the peas left scattered on his plate, attempting to divine some meaning from the pattern. Was Mr. Gerhardt out there?

His mother thought it all a crock. She also occasionally skipped church, citing mysterious headaches.

After dinner, finally allowed to talk, they bobbed for apples in the backyard.

Three white boys in miniature Stetsons, chaps, plaid *bandito* kerchiefs, sagging holsters. One straddled a pony-headed broomstick. Another wore a doll on his left hand, the slit cut into its back pinching the boy's fist like a wrong glove. The doll, too, made up like a cowpoke, its somewhat feminine features obscured by a low-slung hat and a bushy mustache fashioned of trimmed paintbrush bristles.

"Look, Tucson," one of the boys said. "An Injun."

Jalacy, toting a leather knapsack, warily slowed his pace.

"I think that's the Injun that scalped my cousin," Tucson replied, maneuvering his horse so that its head pointed at Jalacy like the barrel of a cannon.

The boys referred to themselves as the 'Skeeters, after the Three Mesquiteers, a popular cowboy trio of the day. Lullaby Joslin, the chubby, wisecracking 'Skeeter in the pictures, always carried a ventriloquist's dummy (Elmer Sneezewood), hence the repurposed doll.

"Let's get him!" Stoney Brooke (Jalacy's classmate Myron Trimble in real life) menacingly twirled his clothesline lasso; Tucson Smith (Teddy Voss) flipped his pony-headed broomstick, wielding it like a club. *Spoils the illusion,* Jalacy thought, while considering his escape options. They'd never actually tried to do anything, not physical. The threats had become ritual, part of an ongoing game. Jalacy hated them but also wished he could be one of them. Who would turn down membership in a posse? He'd asked, once. Teddy/Tucson had said, "*Three*, dummy. And even if was Twelve Mesquiteers, we'd strap a pistol belt to Myron's dog, first."

Jalacy loved the Mesquiteers as much as anyone, though

if pressed, he would acknowledge a preference for Herbert Jeffrey, "the Bronze Buckaroo," the singing cowboy star of race pictures like *Harlem on the Prairie* and *Harlem Rides the Range*. In particular, Jalacy enjoyed the way Jeffrey always found occasion to burst into song, be it on horseback, beside a campfire, in a poker parlor (a mute nod at the piano player the only thing required for on-time and startlingly precise accompaniment), even during a winded lull in a knife fight (with Mexicans, deep in the contested mine shaft), that corny baritone of his floating above the action, *apart* from it, gliding over the surface, or so it seemed, thanks to the smoothness of his delivery. (Also, perhaps more crucially, to his vocals having obviously been dubbed long after the scene's filming was complete.) Jeffrey wore a white hat and a pencil-thin mustache. When he sang, his eyelids drooped in tandem with the corners of his mouth, making his face seem tethered to his relaxed phrasing.

"Why don't you make a war whoop, Injun? Summon your Injun friends. They'll just fall into our trap."

"Call up a spirit animal, Injun."

"Lasso him to a tree."

"Tie him to the horse with the lasso and drag him back to jail."

"Tie him up with the lasso and burn him at the stake."

"Cowboys don't do burnings at the stake."

"Shut up, Injun."

"Indians don't even speak English. Why are you spoiling everything?"

"My parents speak—"

"Back in *old times*, we're talking about."

Jalacy calculated the distance to the mouth of the alley,

which spilled onto Hawthorne, where potential witnesses would be afoot. Unfortunately, he was not the fastest runner.

"Why do they call them Blackfeet?"

"Color of their moccasins, dummy. Everybody knows that."

"This one's wearing brown boots."

"Clever disguise."

"Not clever enough."

Sometimes, while the boys teased him, Jalacy imagined himself as the Bronze Buckaroo. In his mind, he might whip out his six-shooter, or else decide the Mesquiteers deserved a break and simply deliver them a savage beating with his own two fists.

"What do *you* think, Elmer?" Louis Pascoe, as Lullaby, asked his dummy.

Louis was no ventriloquist, so to distract he made his Elmer voice a demented falsetto.

"*Ah dunno, Lullaby!*" Louis-as-Elmer shrieked, puppet-hand bobbing and mouth clearly moving. "*Maybe we oughtta scalp him with his own tomahawk!*"

Louis was a poor choice for the role of Lullaby, the comic relief in the Three Mesquiteer pictures, as he was the most sadistic of the boys and almost never funny. Continuing as Elmer, he began to detail the grisly surgery required to remove Jalacy's scalp, which would eventually be cut into the shape of a false beard and sideburns and worn as a disguise by Louis/Lullaby at Jalacy's funeral.

Teddy and Myron exchanged troubled glances. Louis noticed and said in his own voice, "You're sick, Elmer. Why don't you shut up now. Just shut the hell up."

Jalacy remembered the time the Bronze Buckaroo, cornered in a poker hall by a group of tough hombres, started singing about how he was outnumbered and outgunned. The singing distracted the hombres, buying the Buckaroo enough time for his trusty white horse, Starburst, to kick over a lantern and set the neighboring barn on fire.

As the smoke poured into the saloon, the Bronze Buckaroo was able to shoot his opponents and make his escape.

"Solo Flight." "Pygmy Stomp." "I'd Love to Be Loved." "Assiduously." "Only Foolin'." "Wishing on an Angel." "Handsome Loon." "I'll Take Cash." "I Might Have to Cut the Line." "Nice Try, Nora." "We Didn't Do It (But We Dug It)." "Billable Hours." "Bootleg Rye." "Veni, Vidi, Vera."

Sundays after church, Jalacy's father would sometimes drive the family onto the lake. This only happened in winter, of course. Jalacy's mother packed sandwiches or cold chicken, along with a missile-sized thermos of cocoa, all distributed once the Studebaker had come to a rest at a spot deemed scenic by her husband. After the meal, the chill would be tested with a careful stretch of the legs, and then the young ones skatelessly shuffled sloppy figure eights across the frozen surface until their mother's mittens, clapped together like chalkboard erasers, signaled it was time to go home. His father would never be the first to suggest leaving.

One Sunday Jalacy became convinced he'd heard the ice begin to crack. Sliding back to the car, where his parents remained seated up front, sharing a cigarette but otherwise not speaking, he rapped on the window. His father lowered the glass and asked what was wrong. When Jalacy told him, his father, smiling, explained how the hard winter had left the ice several feet thick, "probably thicker than you're tall," so there was nothing to worry about.

"In fact," his father went on, "statistically we're safer out here than back in the city." Gesturing at the horizon, he said, "I mean, at least we can see our enemies coming."

Jalacy's mother rolled her eyes.

The boy, having already shoved off from the Studebaker, couldn't help thinking, as he launched himself into a wobbly corkscrew and squinted at the distant, blurry tundras spinning beyond his misty breath, how his father, kidding around or not, just might have a point.

On his first day of class at the Cleveland Institute of Music, Jalacy sat beside a twitchy and odd-looking boy named Wendell Jones. Wendell played the oboe. He was skinny to the point of emaciation, with bony elbows that stuck out and quivered excitedly when he blew. The elbows looked as if they'd been broken and then improperly reset. "Your elbows have knuckles," one of the harpists matter-of-factly observed. Jalacy frowned at her, but Wendell paid little attention to the remark, as if he'd long settled into a comfortable resting state of not being particularly well liked. He also had a fixed squint, and the skin all around the edges of his mouth and eyes comprised a series of parched desert states.

The new students sat at long mess tables in a windowless limestone hall. Jalacy, riding to school on the crosstown city bus, had been able to spot a handful of his future classmates, or at least the nonpianists, all toting their instrument cases, the flutes and violins and French horns nimbly so, projecting a fleet-footed confidence, while the flushed, sweaty luggers of cello or tuba appeared predestined to careers of drudgery. An alarming number of his fellow students were not fellows at all, but girls. Jalacy, already made shy and anxious by the commute, felt unprepared for their torturous presence.

"Who do you feel is the most overrated of the so-called great pianists?" Wendell asked Jalacy that morning, after learning his instrument. He spoke with the awkward formality of a radio announcer. Jalacy had no answer, but Wendell did not seem to mind.

"Tabuteau, that diseased animal, is the worst oboe player alive," he said.

It was true, though: his elbows could pass for a boxer's ugly fists.

Konrad Broch, the founder of the conservatory, based his pedagogical approach largely on the fashionable "eurhythmic" method of his fellow Swiss, Dalcroze, whose holistic theory of rhythm emphasized a deep, near-yogic consciousness of all bodily movement as a necessary first step in one's musical development—in essence, a belief that, before coaxing music from another "body," one must recognize the inherent musicality of one's own, "the natural song of a body in motion."

During his introductory remarks, Broch projected slides from various nature studies of human locomotion—those famous images, captured by the early photographer-scientists, of nude men wrestling, tugging ropes, passing tetherballs, ascending and descending inclines, hurling javelins. If observed in daily life, Broch noted, such tasks would not so much as turn a head. And yet, he continued, consider how, when so cataloged and frozen, each step radiates its own beauty—that of a pinned butterfly, of something encapsuled, the sort of beauty evident when the viewer is finally given the time to microscopically examine a wing's thinnest vein.

In keeping with Broch's emphasis on movement, the curriculum at the conservatory included a mandatory ballet course, which Jalacy, though he liked to dance in front of the radio, on those rare occasions his parents and sisters left him alone in the house and he could turn up the latest jitterbug tune as loud as he liked, did not cheerfully anticipate.

"Is there not also something inherently tragic about a leg frozen on an upward swing?" asked Broch, speaking rhetorically. "Such naked striving, cast in amber. The struggle evident in even so simple a human undertaking as"—here he signaled the projector's operator, who advanced the next slide—"*Nude Man Ascending an Incline*. Not a mountain, mind you; a very gentle slope!" These photographic studies of movement, according to Broch, were actually studies of desire. The most mundane of desires, certainly: the desire to climb a staircase, toss a ball, roll a pair of dice, loop one's arm over one's head. "But proof, nonetheless," Broch continued, "that all movement is a form of desire. And is not the awareness of this fact the very definition of dance? Of music? *Of all art?*"

The conservatory had been his parents' idea. Though Jalacy had happily agreed to the suggestion, he still had trouble thinking of music in terms of a possible calling. Music lovers who have no facility for playing themselves have a tendency to assign an almost sacramental vocation (wild-eyed, in the manner of Mozart) to all musicians, when in fact, one (passion) does not necessarily follow the other (talent); certainly with Jalacy, his voracious appetite for music of every style (opera had become his latest obsession) had yet to translate into any sort of deep urgency to create his own. But the ability, certainly, was there—Jalacy could pick out all but the most complex songs on the piano after only a couple of listens. And so the conservatory made practical sense. How else would he satisfy his desire to live with music, to be around it constantly?

He'd started to fool around with his voice, even back then. "One day," he told his friends, "I might be the next Paul Robeson. The next Enrico Caruso."

The outbreak of the war would make his musical studies feel increasingly frivolous.

Weekends, Jalacy and Wendell began working as junior

ushers down at the opera house. The job involved polishing brass fixtures before the show, sweeping up after.

Broch, that first day, pacing the aisles of the lecture room, asked the class, "And who do you think *created* music?" Jalacy, at that moment, made the mistake of expectantly meeting the instructor's gaze. He'd assumed the question had been another rhetorical, the answer forthcoming. Broch took the eye contact as a provocation. "Who do you think created music?" he repeated, now, suddenly looming over Jalacy and glaring down at him with a terrifying intensity. Jalacy still did not immediately process the question as real. He stole a glance at Wendell, who, unhelpfully, was now studying his notebook as if consumed by a difficult but intriguing math puzzle. "Well?" Broch thundered. "It must have been some-body. Was it the angels?" Jalacy said no. "Who, then?" Broch asked. "Was it the monkeys?" Broch leaned over Jalacy and, puffing his cheeks, began to scratch at his own armpits with apeish uncoordination, at the same time screeching, "Eeep! Eeep! Eeep!" Jalacy stared back at him and mumbled, "That's not music." Broch, dropping his arms, smiled and said, "Good."

[Chuckles.]

Hours I spent here, as an impressionable youth. Right . . .
[Squints up at balcony.]

Well. Somewhere up there. Junior usher, high school.
"Una furtiva lagrima" comes from *L'elisir d'amore*, an opera
by Donizetti I first saw performed on this very stage. It's
about a love potion, you know. Sound familiar?

*[Whistles "I Put a Spell on You" as he makes his way across
the stage to a prop throne, where he takes a seat.]*

More like it, eh? Now, where was I? Oh, right: my appreciation for the fine arts. Well, you know, I started on the
piano, back when I was still wearing short pants. Later, I
picked up the sax. Can't say when the idea to sing first took
possession of my thick skull. On one level, it's elementary
psychology, I guess. The abandoned, always craving the
world's embrace. The ham, forever seeking the king's plate.
Who can say? What I do know is, while I listened to everything, opera struck me, by far, as the most exotic. And I don't
just mean the music, which I took to, immediately, raptur-
ously. I'm talking about the damned stories! The chief usher
had a rule: no thumbing through the programs while on the
clock. So most of the time, I had no idea what was supposed
to be happening down here. I think I started enjoying the
mystery, to be honest. Added to the strangeness of the music.
I had fun coming up with my own plots. For some reason, I
became convinced that *Aida* was set entirely in Florida. *Otello*
I interpreted as a ghost story. Made sense! Desdemona flitting
about the stage in that white gown, her every appearance
seeming to further derange and terrify the Moor: I had to
stop myself from hooting when Otello finally strangled the
hideous creeper!

CHAPTER THREE

A Boyhood Love of Opera

[*A theater curtain rises to reveal a painted pastoral backa... various dusty props. A supertitle flashes above the proscen... BOYHOOD LOVE OF OPERA. Hawkins, in full costume, em... from the wings and gazes around the set. Finally, he turns to ... audience and seems to force a smile.*]

Are you familiar with "Una furtiva lagrima"? *A furtive teardrop.* Very famous aria. I could hum it, and you'd recognize the tune.

[*Hums aria.*]

That one. Nemorino, a heartsick peasant, is the tenor. He's convinced the girl wants no part of him. She has agreed to marry the boorish sergeant.

Something I always wanted to do, but never did, is sing opera. But when I got into the business, opera didn't make it onto the charts. They were just putting rhythm and blues out.

[*Wanders back into the set and picks up prop sword.*]

Wonder who this belonged to?

[*Blows dust from length of sword, gently, as if playing scales on a flute.*]

I'm going to guess . . . Siegfried? I'm feeling a certain Wagnerian heft.

[*Makes halfhearted en garde.*]

Although, on the other hand, suppose it could be Falstaff's.

[*Begins to sing, assuming parodic trill.*]

Tutto nel mondo è burla!

Hawkins' one-man show, *Baptize Me in Wine*, ran at the Zipper Factory Theater in New York City for two months in 1984.

[*Abruptly stands and walks over to laden banquet table.*]

Anyone hungry? I am famished.

[*Lifts dome from silver serving platter, revealing, beneath, a prop severed head.*]

Aha! Well, one mystery solved.

[*Picks up head by hair and holds it close to his own face, examining it.*]

I would not have guessed *Salome*. I used to learn those songs phonetically, you know. The opera tunes. Drove my folks crazy. Of course, I tended to pick the most bombastic numbers. Always had a good memory for anything set to music. Once the show got started, most of the ushers went down to the basement to play euchre, smoke. Not me. I'd just stand back in the shadows, behind the last row of seats in the uppermost balcony. Back there in the shadows, mouthing along to words I didn't know, trailing a half beat behind the singer. Tracing just outside the line.

[*Stares severed head directly in the eye for a moment before turning back to the audience.*]

In *L'elisir d'amore*, Nemorino purchases an "elixir of love" to win the heart of Adina, a rich landowner who by all social rules of the day shouldn't have been on our guy's radar. Unfortunately, what he's been sold turns out to be a jug of cheap wine, passed off as a magic potion by a quack doctor. Still, the elixir has its desired effect: Nemorino becomes drunken and winds up cavorting with the village women, and when Adina spies him dancing with someone else, she's finally prompted to reveal her own feelings by allowing that *furtiva lagrima* to roll down her cheek. Now, for some reason, first time *yours truly* watched these scenes unfold, I missed the bit where Nemorino swigs from the jug, and so I decided it must be a funeral urn. "Someone die?" I whispered to a fellow usher, a retired truck driver named Carlton. "Ya," he hissed, "his uncle." Nemorino's revelry, in this mistaken context, struck me as morbid and inappropriate.

Later, of course, after he sees that furtive teardrop, Nemorino swells up with joy. He's finally been given undeniable proof of Adina's reciprocated love. Though in certain respects it's a perverted joy, because it depends on the misery, however temporary, of his beloved. And when he sings the aria in question, he sounds pretty miserable himself. Maybe he's touched by her own sadness. Or maybe he's a clownish drunk, weeping happy-sad tears.

[*Shrugs.*]

I thought it had to do with the dead uncle.

[*Replaces severed head on serving tray and steps away from table.*]

Always reminded me of the story of Jesus in the garden. "Una furtiva lagrima," I mean: the delivery of the song. Nemorino stands alone, at this point, the fawning peasant girls having all drifted away.

[*Lights dim, shrouding the backdrop until he becomes a lone figure, surrounded by utter darkness.*]

He's so ecstatic. His true love is weeping . . . for him! And yes, you could describe Christ's experience as opposite. Jesus wept for himself, out of *fear*, while his useless disciples dozed. I suppose it was Nemorino's solitude that conjured Gethsemane for me. That, and the song itself. "Una furtiva lagrima" *is* a prayer to the Father, after all. One of thanks, not desperation, true.

[*The faint light on his figure brightens, setting him off from the darkness.*]

But sure sounded like desperation to me. I can still remember that tenor's face, as he stood on this very stage. Maybe the pain of holding those notes made him look so tortured. Maybe it was a deliberate acting choice. But suddenly, for me? Whatever broad farce I thought I'd been watching transformed itself into something else entirely.

[*Sings.*]

Cielo, si può morir, di più non chiedo.

[*Speaking voice, again.*]

"Oh God, I will die. I cannot ask for more."

From happiness, I didn't realize at the time.

[*Lights come up abruptly. The speaker appears startled.*]

CHAPTER FOUR

Army Years

Jalacy, at fourteen, had never ridden in a train, glimpsed the ocean, journeyed more than two states beyond Ohio, been intimate with a member of the opposite sex, boarded a ship, fired a rifle, cracked a coconut, forgotten to take his antimalarial medication, explosively shat in the presence of grown men, experienced "prickly heat" (or, for that matter, the company of an underage prostitute), smoked a cigarette, tasted rum, noted the shape of New Guinea on a map, heard of the Kumbai tribesmen, or spent any noteworthy amount of time with adult males who were not his adopted Indian father or music teacher.

To Jalacy, these men possessed a confidence, above all else. Their personalities and mannerisms felt immutable, indigenous, and they moved with a lack of the needling self-consciousness he couldn't shake. He constantly reviewed his own performances, subjected them to merciless critiques: the missed opportunities, the mute intimidation. Flinching at a toucan squawk, at a sudden change in the light. And his body, all of *those* changes. The constant, incorrigible boners.

What the hell was he going to become?

The shape of the island was a bird.

He had never worried about getting dysentery. He had never tasted Spam.

The yellow Atabrine pills prevented malaria but caused nightmares. Jalacy, who never remembered his dreams back home, thrashed about his bunk as if beset by fever or biting insects. The insect-biting often turned out to be real, it being the jungle after all, though in the nightmares, more familiar creatures tended to torment his dream-self: wasps, alley rats, their Cleveland neighbors' nervous chow Wong.

He had never seen a Japanese soldier up close.

Basic training had not left him adequately prepared for combat or jungle. Or so it appeared, from his perspective. The all-colored units had been made to train with substandard weaponry, for the most part leftovers from the previous war, heavy equipment with outmoded parts, prone to strange rattles. Privates reflexively averted their faces before squeezing a trigger, hoping to shield at least one eye, just in case. Even the stuffed dummies they charged during infantry practice leaked hay. The white unit's mule mascot periodically wandered onto the field for a nibble. Nobody said he couldn't.

He had never encountered the charms of the Australian accent, let alone heard it shouted from a motorcycle sidecar while applied to sentences like *Watch your back, nigger!* He had ejaculated onto his own stomach, on a number of occasions, but never with a Fijian prostitute grasping his penis and working her hand rhythmically and mechanically along its length (well, "length") as if she were performing a legitimate medical procedure. Jalacy, that first time, had concentrated on his own deep embarrassment at having the men who had brought him to the brothel cheering his passage into the designated boudoir as if he'd just sprinted past a petty officer, first class at an Army-Navy track meet. He'd found he preferred to keep others ignorant of his desires, which to him felt like weaknesses, brayed deficiencies.

The bored look on the girl's face was a whorehouse cliché, he would later come to learn, one which certain men considered a part of the titillation. The act of abandon gelded of passion, turned mundane, a sort of extra perversity all its own.

* * *

Jalacy had not been the first underage applicant to turn up in Lieutenant Duffy's downtown Cleveland enlistment office in 1943. A dearth of options on the home front, combined with the not-inconsiderable patriotic fervor of the day, made Jalacy and a number of others close to his age, many having joined the workforce years earlier, act with adult determination upon their rash, adolescent impulse to run off with other boys, to run *toward* the explosion. Duffy presided over a dull gunmetal desk, a bright new flag hanging gratuitously behind him. Certain fat men look as if they're holding their breath when they attempt a stern or pensive expression; so the lieutenant, sizing up young Jalacy over a pair of reading glasses. "Sizing," literally, at least in part: Lieutenant Duffy seemed to be trying to picture whether or not the smallest of the standard-issue army helmets might swallow Jalacy's head too noticeably, like a serving bowl worn at a party for comic effect, making his own credulity seem either willful or idiotic.

Jalacy allowed his eyes to dart to his enlistment papers, thus far ignored, though assertively flattened, nearly covered, in fact, by a fleshy, splay-fingered hand. The lieutenant, shifting in his seat, cocked his gaze, as if appraising a sculpture from different angles. His glasses perched on the edge of his nose, the lenses empty windows pointing blankly in the direction of the papers. Jalacy had a sudden urge to snatch a writing implement from the desk's pen-and-pencil vase and trace an outline of Lieutenant Duffy's hand, then wondered if such thoughts made him too childish for military service.

"March," Jalacy told the enlistment officer. Despite his best efforts at approximating adultspeak, his voice sounded, to his own ears, distant and reedy, like it was being funneled through a crude amplification device constructed of coffee cans. "Eighteen this past March."

Duffy absorbed the boy's birthdate with no visible reaction. "You sure of that, son?" he finally asked, his voice remaining flat and unaffected.

Jalacy told himself not to fidget, to maintain the posture of the piano bench. Hands limp, lapbound. Feet flat, tracing parallel lines.

"My mother always said I had a baby's face, sir," he said. He tried to harden his features by force of will.

Duffy nodded silently. Jalacy wasn't sure if he should continue to meet the lieutenant's gaze. That might seem a provocation, the brazen stare of an insubordinate. Though, alternately, glancing into his lap could be interpreted as weak and unbefitting of a soldier.

Duffy's chin folds bunched at his neck like a tucked napkin.

Jalacy had never felt entirely tethered to his adopted parents. Surely the lack of blood ties, and the unignorable dissimilarities in pigmentation, sowed confusion in the boy; throughout his childhood, he had a persistent, if vague, notion that he might, at any moment, without notice or consequence, be snatched away from the family of which he'd been made a gift. Which certainly eased this departure of his own volition. He'd had years to mentally prepare. While awaiting his turn at Duffy's desk, Jalacy found, in fact, that he felt no anxiety at the prospect of separation from his parents, nor distress at the concomitant hurt and betrayal his leaving would necessarily stir. His prime concern remained purely mechanical, how most painlessly to break the news of his enlistment. (Eventually, he settled upon a short note.)

They talked, some, about the conservatory. It turned out Duffy had played the trumpet. Strictly amateur, not even talented enough, by his own admission, to make the cut in the army band.

"I can hit any note you put in front of me, but I could never really swing," Duffy said. "That has always been my shortcoming."

Jalacy nodded, glancing again at those big hands. Duffy had a pianist's reach, but the fat fingers would have made his playing worthless. When Jalacy mentioned Glenn Miller's enlistment, Duffy snarled, "That four-eyed woodchopper," whipping off his own glasses, consciously or not, as a rhetorical flourish. They debated Miller versus Duke for at least ten minutes, with Jalacy finding himself in the odd position of defending the populist appeal of the former's arrangements, citing, in particular, Tex Beneke's sax solo on "(I've Got a Gal in) Kalamazoo." Duffy snorted and said, "Exceptions prove shit, even rotten organizations have design flaws, by which I mean the fact that nothing is thoroughly lousy does not lessen the lousiness inherent and undeniable in said thing."

Finally, his rubber stamp hovering pregnantly above Jalacy's application, the lieutenant said, "You understand, now, son, the likelihood of your getting assigned to an army band is actually quite slim?"

"Of course," Jalacy replied.

Secretly, though, he had a notion he might manage to sneak into the rhythm section, at least. Things seemed to be going his way.

* * *

"Opera, huh?"

Mickels, his bunkmate. First night in country, after chow. Jalacy on the floor, legs in a swami position. Absently lacing a boot.

"I like it."

"You a dago or something? Sarge told me you were a Red Indian."

"I like all kinds of music."

"Hey! Ya-huh-ha. Hey! Ya-huh-ha. Hey! Ya-huh-ha."

Mickels, not bothering to accompany his sound effect with the appropriate mouth percussion or cyclone dance, remained sprawled on his belly, the dramatization of his exhaustion clearly improving his mood.

"You ever been to a powwow?"

"No."

"I have. Outside Albuquerque."

"Lots of Indians out that way."

"I feel like these might have been Mexicans, painted up to look like Indians."

"That's a sneaky trick."

"For a buck. What people will do. How old are you, really, Junior?"

"Seventeen and a half."

"Come on, kid. Don't insult me."

Jalacy didn't answer. Mickels flipped onto his back, began fingering his dog tag the way certain of the Italian mama's boys did their crosses. With his other hand, he extended an index finger and began tracing inscrutable letters upon the mosquito netting billowing over his mattress.

"So, an enlisted man, huh? You some kind of patriot?"

"No more than you, I suppose."

"Couldn't wait to put the tomahawk to old Jerry."

"We all do our part."

"Adventure. Excitement. See the world."

"Maybe, partwise."

"Cheapest ticket out of South Bend."

"Cleveland. Sure, man. You reading me like a magazine."

"What'd your folks say?"

"Didn't tell 'em. Not until I'd made it down to basic."

"Just slipped right out one night?"

"Boy who walked through walls."

"I wasn't drafted? You'd be whistling solo right now."

"Ha ha. I don't believe that."

"Believe it."

Jalacy slipped under the netting of his own bunk. It helped, some, though one morning he'd woken to find a giant slug, the shape and color of an extracted tonsil, affixed to one of the knuckles of his right hand.

"So they try to stop you?"

"Nah. They dropped me a postcard."

"Postcard?"

"Picture of the Terminal Tower on the front."

" 'Buddy won't come out from under the porch since you been gone, he misses you so.' That kind of thing?"

"They said the lake was still too cold to swim."

" 'Pawpaw's beside himself. He started talking to the cows.' "

"The lake temperature was about it. I grew up in the city, not on a farm."

"'Conky Bill and Jimmy the Box Cutter got pinched for armed robbery. Lucky you made it off the block, kiddo.'"

"My mother wrote the card and signed everyone's name."

"Huh." Mickels lay quiet for a moment. Finally, he went on, "That's okay. I hate my folks, too."

"I don't hate my folks."

"No, course not."

"I had a wonderful childhood."

Mickels began to violently flail at his netting.

"I feel like a trout!"

Someone from another bunk yelled, "Maybe I should club you against the side of the boat."

Jalacy said, "I don't hate them."

Mickels sucked his cheeks in and made his lips pucker open and closed, like a fish's mouth, one choking on air. A couple of the fellow privates chuckled, though not Jalacy, who couldn't see Mickels' face from the bunk below.

Mostly his time in the Pacific involved the patrolling of a couple of landing strips at the end of the base. Long before he'd arrived, they'd cleared out a grove of banyan trees with bulldozers and laid tarmac. Molasses sap, ground coral. The importance of the patrols could not be underestimated, according to their CO, who insisted Jap control of air traffic at this end of the island would mean an obscure yet cruel advantage. The specific manner of attack remained unknown. The COs were mum on such details, though Jalacy, squinting fitfully at the lush overgrowth, scraping away forehead sweat with the sharp backside of a wrist, half expected Jap faces to suddenly materialize, miragelike, in the chlorophyll haze.

"They have the silence," murmured Mickels one night. "Not like us, man. We can't keep it to ourselves."

"What do you mean, the silence?"

"It's Oriental."

Jalacy shifted his gun's barrel from left hand to right shoulder, then back again. It felt like he was hoisting a two-by-four. This Pacific heat weighed you down. They didn't tell you how it burrowed under your skin like chiggers, made you feel wrapped in a damp but coarse gauze. They didn't tell you about the jungle noise, a steady, humming symphony of birds and cicadas and God knew what other manner of tropical critter, their low, mind-clearing drone fit to rival any monkish dirge, only stretched thin, draping the entire island like a net, come nightfall.

The thin, pressurized whine of a tea kettle just on the cusp, always seeming ready to blow. And what would happen then? Would the animals pour forth from the jungle, hysterical gymnastic chimps baring their gums and shrieking, or dark-armored insects, spreading across the ground like spilled oil, a sudden shadow? Throw in the native population, those furious pole-vaulters gripping their spears with both hands. Last thing he'd ever see.

That or the Japs.

They paced their end of the airstrip, Jalacy and Field, a country boy from Alabama. His actual name was Hudson, Field being short for Left Field, on account of his mouth having the unfortunate tendency to hang open, regardless of whether he was speaking or not. (He was always catching flies, get it?) They called Jalacy "Junior," for obvious reasons.

Occasionally Jalacy would remove his helmet, drop it on the strip, use it as a humped seat.

"You look like you're riding a turtle, Junior."

Jalacy said not to taunt him with such excitement, it was mean.

His uniform never quite fit properly. He had to keep the sleeves folded over, making his arms feel thick-ended and unwieldy. His pants ballooned out from under his tightened belt, skirtish and loose, boots jutting like a clown's. Only thing he lacked was a seltzer bottle, handkerchief, maybe a cane. Although his rifle could be a potentially funny prop.

They paced their end nightly, until relief arrived. Occasionally a signal for a plane came in. Field said *single*, a source of much amusement for the rest of the squad. But that was just his pronunciation. Jalacy thought he was basically a clever guy.

They did make a funny pair. Jalacy, with his kid's face, which, you had to stand close enough to kiss him to even spy a stray whisker or two, stickmen curling to earth like cowerers from their own loneliness. And flanking the boy, nearly doubling him, Field looking like he might have been thumb-pressed out of dough.

"You up-North fellows can't hack this," Field said one night, snickering at Jalacy's visible discomfort at the heat. "For a southern fellow? This is just August."

Jalacy nodded hotly, his own mouth hanging open, hoping to air out the complex. He took a step off the tarmac, into the wet grass. It had rained that afternoon, as it had every after-noon since they had come ashore on this sodden isle, regular as church bells. You'd think all the moisture would cool things off, but it just called up more steam. Jalacy watched his boot sink into the wet grass, the pressure causing pools of muddy water to rise and flood the stalks immediately surrounding the area of impact. He lifted his boot and the water dropped, then planted it again with a squishy authority, reflooding the miniature field, a reverse colander effect.

You had to watch out for certain types of grass, as illus-trated in the manual they'd been given upon arrival. Tall and sharp, these stalks would slice you to bleeding, according to the soldiers who'd bothered to actually read it. Blades, for real.

Japs supposedly had the power to pass through them without getting so much as a nick. Some means of concen-trated walking. That was not in the manual.

Field took a swig from his canteen, the water inside making a satisfying slosh, both hollow and metallic, a wet per-cussion. Jalacy stared at his boots. They'd marched them so hard during basic, he'd had to peel his socks off and wring out the blood.

Field sang softly, *I'll be effing you, in all the old familiar places*. Mickels' rewrite, composed a few weeks back.

In the can and in the mouth, between your—Field clicked his tongue in country-boy censorship of the bluer lyrics—*and further south . . .*

Everyone considered foot patrol a much worse duty. Jalacy had drawn a handful. They'd wound up criss-crossing half the island, picking their way along overgrown trails, choking on the rotting, overripe stink that permeates a jungle, ducking vines mistook for snakes, getting razzed for doing so, hacking a real king cobra to pieces with a machete. Jalacy did not do the hacking, personally.

I'll be looking at Muldoon—here Mickels had added, in a spoken-word aside Field chose to omit, "Muldoon, you really oughtta shave that back of yours"—*but I'll be screwin' youuuuuu.*

Field cut the elongated *you* short. Just a bit, but enough to make Jalacy look up from his boot.

"What?"

"Hear something?"

They both fell silent.

"No. You?"

Something rustled. They both raised their rifles, Jalacy feeling his own whipping upward like another limb, an instinctual motion. He might have been raising a palm to block a punch, break a fall. This both scared him and made him proud. He couldn't hear anything else out of the ordinary.

Jalacy glanced at Field. The big man looked afraid, but he nodded at the tangle of shadow and leaves, first to his edge of the tarmac, on the east side, then to Jalacy's. Jalacy gave him a reciprocal nod and began moving toward the jungle, rifle pointing the way, stepping as noiselessly as possible, willing himself to glide. Ears tweaked, trying to recall the various animals illustrated in the manual. Could be a lemur. They had glowing eyes, so would be easy to spot.

On the tarmac, the moonlight had provided deceptively soothing illumination, at once sharp-edged and hushed. But once Jalacy had stepped a few feet into the brush, he found himself smothered by a terrifying darkness. He paused, waiting for his sight to adjust.

He could move forward, or stand still and listen, or retrace his footsteps backward, waving his gun like a chastising finger. *No. No. No. You. Better. Not. Follow.* He chose the second option. He wanted to call out Field's name. Why did they have to be silent, if they were, in theory, the ones being crept upon? Why had he listened to that big dumb bastard and marched into the jungle in the middle of the night?

Cold blade against his jugular. A whisper: Japanese for, *Be still.*

Or the opposite, a bright flash, blinding, the roar of artillery discharge now so familiar and yet equally startling, and the pain, they said it hurt to be shot, but no one told you exac—

Jalacy froze. He'd never seen a Kumbai tribesman before, outside of the photographs in the manual. This one, lit by a streak of moonlight that had pierced the canopy of the jungle, wore no mask. He was bare-chested, shoeless, his penis sheathed and curving up slightly, like the horn of a billy goat, or a longish mollusk. The sheath seemed to be woven from bamboo and banyan leaves.

"Junior!" Field called out in a hoarse whisper, from somewhere in the blackness.

The Kumbai stood perfectly still, a diorama in a natural history museum. Polished white shells, triple the size of pearls on a necklace, hung heavily from a crowded string, resting upon the tribesman's shoulders more like a wreath. A septet of hornbill beaks poked from his wild hair like antlers, while an unidentifiable bone, long and thin, threaded his flared, oddly regal septum, either sharpened end broadly orbiting the base of his chin in the manner of an elaborately waxed mustache.

Jalacy could barely breathe, though he had a gun and the Kumbai was defenseless.

"Junior!"

He was not the enemy.

And then Jalacy experienced something wholly unexpected—what could only be described as a "waking vision." In an instant, he'd left the suffocating heat of the jungle and found himself standing on the stage of a grand theater. The backdrop had been painted to resemble a jungle air base, and men dressed as soldiers, arranged like a chorus, stood around him in formation. His own army uniform, however, had vanished and been replaced by the tribal costume of the Kumbai. In the audience, white couples in formal dress gazed upon the scene with an air of expectancy. Some used opera glasses. Jalacy glanced down at his newly sheathed cock, lightly fingering his shelled collar, his bone mustache, the bird parts nestled in his hair. They expected him to sing. But he had no sense of which opera he'd been thrust into, let alone his role. Panicked, he closed his eyes, thinking back to his time at the conservatory. Could there be an obvious candidate he'd entirely forgotten? Nothing came to mind. (Exactly one afternoon at the conservatory had been devoted to a discussion of Negro music, critiquing an "appreciation" of jazz written by a Swiss conductor named Ernest Ansermet.)

And then, in a sudden rush, he had the aria. Along with the opera as a whole, which told the story of his own life: Cleveland, the war, his Indian parents, his dreams of a musical career. He also saw later acts, hazier ones, featuring nightclubs, women, flamboyant men screaming into microphones. A tropical beach. A coffin. The words to the aria came to him all at once, with a beautiful melody, which the musicians in the orchestra pit immediately struck up, the horn section first, raunchy and aggressive, followed by a sole pianist.

Played aloud, Jalacy had to admit, it did not sound like opera.

Jalacy opened his eyes. He'd returned to the jungle. An agitated Field now stood where the Kumbai had been. "Why didn't you answer me?" he cried. Jalacy, blinking, realized the tribesman must have slipped away. For a moment, he considered carrying on with the aria; he could still remember all of the words.

In the end, however, he decided upon discretion.

Unsung Aria of the Kumbai
(FROM ERNEST ANSERMET)

The blues occurs
When the Negro is sad
When he is far from his home
His mother
Or his sweetheart.
Then he thinks of a motif
Or a preferred rhythm
And takes his trombone
Or his violin
Or his banjo
Or his clarinet
Or his drum
Or else he sings.
Or simply dances.
And on the chosen motif
He plumbs the depths
Of his imagination.
This makes his sadness
Pass away.

It is not
The material
That makes
Negro music.
It is the spirit.

He had never been sick on fried Spam and bananas, nor had he heard of dehydrated eggs, much less seen a nineteen-year-old from Vicco, Kentucky, eat several heaping spoonfuls of yellow powder and then declare, "All the same to me." He had never been sick from watching another person eat.

Several of the guys played guitar, one or two exceptionally well, and quiet nights, sitting around the bunk tent, songs would get passed around, mostly down-home blues or Tin Pan Alley standards. Mickels managed to requisition a horn for the "Yuletide Follies" show that first Christmas, colored lights hooked to a generator bejeweling skinny coconut trees like a rich lady's arm, medi-unit-cotton snowdrifts, some of the boys in makeshift drag doing Lena Horne doing "White Christmas," Carmen Miranda, Fredi Washington's monologue from *Imitation of Life*, Josephine Baker. Mickels, having exaggerated his own skills, which more or less ended after a few passable honks, quickly lost interest in the show and bequeathed his instrument to Junior. The pads on the saxophone, ravaged by the local humidity, had come to pieces, but Jalacy snagged a few rubber bands from the supply closet and was able to keep the thing from falling apart. It was a tenor, and though it was his first time fooling around with a sax, he came to love its shrill insistence.

He had never heard of, nor helped to load, an "electric donkey," basically a mining cart attached to a motor-powered pulley, making it easier to transport munitions, foodstuffs, and various other supplies from trucks at the base of a hill up and over to a second set of trucks waiting to convoy the loot to their own base. The afternoons were unbearable. Most of the men on electric-donkey duty removed their shirts and rolled up their pant legs. Dog tags dangled and swung, a light counterpoint to the physical exertions, occasionally catching the sun just right and sending out fiery little darts. Jalacy felt muffled by the heat, pressed on all sides. He performed the lifting and sliding mechanically, without thought, attempting to detach his brain from the operation.

He had never heard nor sung of Jody, who seemed to have gotten into the pants of everyone's sweetheart. He hadn't realized there wasn't no use in goin' home ('cause Jody got her out on loan), or that he'd best forget about that gal in Mississipp' ('cause Jody givin' her a little tip), ditto Spokane (she experiencing Jody's élan), South Bend (check her mouth, friend), and San Berdoo (her man ain't you).

Mickels had a thin mustache, which he rather fussily attended to, his face cocked in front of the little mirror hanging from his bunk as he performed delicate procedures with a miniature brush and quarter-bladed scissors. He had a story about a couple of buddies, maybe six months back, who'd heard something while on jungle patrol and stopped dead in their tracks. It turned out to be Artie Shaw and his band playing "Begin the Beguine." Shaw had enlisted in the navy and been sent to the Pacific, where he'd put together a group. They were practicing their set, Shaw, being such an insane perfectionist, and knowing the jungle would affect his instruments, needing to hear exactly *how*, and so refusing to rehearse indoors.

The night at the brothel, Jalacy had sex three times (hand, genitals, hand again), which ultimately didn't take very long, those eager fumblings, as little as he possessed in the ways of age or experience. He spent the rest of the session talking.

The prostitute, close to his own age, did not speak English, so the conversation was more of a monologue.

The girl had puffy downturned lips, chin-length black hair, a head slightly too big for her body, a young boy's absence of feminine curves. The comforter had a leopard design: not leopard print but actual leopards, lolling and stalking about. The walls, painted a watery milkshake brown, displayed various streaks of discoloration, wobbly prison bars dripped from above. A winged ceiling fan could be flapped by yanking on a rope. The girl lazily tugged the knotted end, one-armed, as she sat on her heels directly beneath the main throughway of the manufactured breeze, luxuriating in it, sometimes emitting an exaggerated coo, as if she were sitting in a river.

Jalacy told her she was the prettiest girl he'd seen since he left Cleveland. He said, "We went out in canoes and shot a couple of crocodiles the other day," the "we" a technical truth, if one spoke of the entire troop as a single unit. Jalacy had, personally, never been invited on a hunt (white officers only). He asked her how she stood the mosquitoes. Had her feel his brailled back and limbs, mimed clawing off his own skin. He said the Australians were racist brutes; one, he'd heard, kept a dried, shriveled Jap head dangling from his belt as a lucky charm. He told her about a time in the trench, with Field, when a Jap battleship started raining bombs on their position, and it sounded like a train barreling over them, like they'd squeezed into a gap between the tracks. Grasping each other and hugging the ground, eyes clenched shut, unbelievable rumble above their backs. Jalacy said he'd never been that close, *physically* close, to another human being in his entire life. Not even to his mother, he didn't think.

He had never listened to the radio broadcasts of Tokyo Rose, who, one evening, wondered if her audience ever noticed how the GI stations played nothing but wait-for-me songs: "Till Then," "I'll Be Seeing You," "I'll Be Home for Christmas," "Waitin' for the Train to Come In," "Auf Weidersehen, Sweetheart." There *will* be bluebirds over the white cliffs of Dover. "We'll Meet Again." Will, till, when, comin'. And what, Rose asked, did we think the subtle message might be?

"Nothing subtle," Mickels muttered. "We fucking lonely. That's the message."

What did we think our sweethearts were doing back home, besides working in tank factories, growing beans up the back trellis to feed the children, and looking in, once a week or so, on Mother? Wasn't there something a tad *desperate* about all these hokey tunes? Sure, they can't wait to see you. Keep telling yourself dyat. (Rose's pronunciation occasionally got a bit funky, attempting various regional accents.) Ruth's a real peach. She'd never stray. Penny for your thoughts, Dottie. Except why waste a penny when you get letters from her once a week? Unless you think she's holding out . . .

Then she'd play a tune by Ellington or Coleman Hawkins or Wild Bill Davison. Tokyo Rose had all of the hottest jazz records. It was no contest.

Someone started banging on the door, one of the guys from his unit, yelling for Junior to go easy on the poor girl. How much more did he think she could take?

CHAPTER FIVE

Alaska

It was disconcerting for Jay, who had boxed casually throughout his armed forces career, to become aware of a largely white cheering section in his own corner. By this point, U.S. military focus had shifted to the Cold War, making the proximity of the Alaskan Territory to the Soviet Union of great strategic interest. The awesome, terrifying expanse of Siberia lay just across the Bering Strait, and war exercises took place involving Russian fighter planes banking along the Pacific coast to rain bombs on the Grand Coulee Dam and the plutonium facility in Hanford, all of which ultimately spooked the brass enough to prompt a serious increase in personnel, matériel, and fort and base infrastructure in what would soon become the forty-ninth state. Elmendorf, the old air force base just east of Anchorage where Jay, having reenlisted (and switched branches) after the war, had been stationed, wound up as one of the beneficiaries of this largesse.

It wasn't as though Jay possessed some deep passion for boxing. The sport came easy to him, to be sure, in those days of long-limbed youth, especially. But he never dreamed of being Ezzard Charles or Joe Louis or Archie Moore, never spoke reverently of the "sweet science." In fact, he found himself easily bored when the other guys crowded around a transistor radio to listen to the wooden blow-by-blow of some match at the Garden, with its staticky backdrop of cheers and groans. One of his justifications for acceding to the pressure coming from all quarters to participate in this specific fight had been the presence of an actual purse, which, however meager, could nonetheless be set aside for his entertainment budget.

The match took place at a salmon cannery on the out-skirts of town. Which *outskirts*? Certain words turned funny in Alaska. As Jay prepared to enter the ring, bouncing anticipatorily on the balls of his feet and hidden by a wall of stacked pallets, his breaths lingered in ghostly form. The chatter of the men crowding the ring, eager to spectate, some in folding chairs, most standing, echoed hollowly in the open space. For some reason, Jay recalled a chilly night outside a bar in Seoul. Similar male crowd, milling about. A handwrit-ten sign awkwardly promoted a local attempt at a jazz night: GRIND TIL YOU LOSE YOUR MINE [*sic*]. "Buddhist joint?" Jay's buddy Ledbetter had deadpanned.

Independent of the military base expansion, postwar Alaska had already been experiencing a bit of a boomlet, as a percentage of the millions of returning servicemen, in search of opportunity and, more existentially, inflamed by wander-lust after their first, fleeting tastes of life abroad, struck north, eager to reap the storied riches of the farthest American frontier. Alaska's gold rush days had long passed, but the dis-tant, frozen land retained a certain foreboding mystique, its sheer inaccessibility promising an abundance of rewards long hidden from the lazy and less resourceful. That was the dream being sold, anyway. On a more practical level, if the riches failed to immediately materialize, there were plenty of jobs to be had in the timber, fishing, and oil industries, not to mention construction work on any number of the projects required to accommodate the rapidly growing military presence.

Ledbetter had spent the war in Europe. He came from Harlem. His first name, bequeathed to him at birth, happened to be General, though he'd enlisted as a private, a source of deep amusement to soldiers of every rank. Jay had never been to Paris. Private General Ledbetter liked to go on at length about how the very pigeons over there seemed cleaner—how, compared to the rat-birds of New York, they appeared to have been dusted with the same powder used on those King Louis wigs.

He'd also done his best to talk Jay out of the big fight, citing, variously, the inherent danger of being noticed, the unknownness of his opponent, Billy McCann, and of course the likelihood of some manner of race-hate-driven plot on the part of the peckerwood brass. There had to be a catch, one that would certainly not end well for Hawkins.

Jay had learned to box as a boy, taught by a retired mill worker back in Cleveland. He remembered the way Mr. Earl would slip off his shirt and get down on his knees for a mostly stationary spar with the littlest students, demonstrating various bobs and parries and cover-ups before reaching around with a right hook to give the kid a gentle tap on the side of the head, seemingly indifferent to the rather undignified stumpy shifts of torso circumstances forced him to adopt. "This a for-real fight?" Mr. Earl always asked. "Denny be lying on his back visiting the Taj Mahal right now." Jay also remembered, after working that speed bag, the way the dull muscle-ache in his shoulders and forearms had started to pinch him like a tight sweater, and how, despite the obvious upleasantness, he'd been surprised to find that he kind of liked it, that feeling of constriction. Something oddly cozy about the pain.

What was known of Billy McCann, middleweight champion of Alaska, was that he was nearly thirteen years Hawkins' senior, a member of the electrical workers' union who had come to the backcountry to work on the pipeline. No one could say for certain why they called him "Billy the Bawler." Cook insisted it had something to do with the crazed, animalistic way he'd sweat, which approximated a teariness during latter stages of the bout, while Biondo said no, his *eyes* would actually get a little moist, to the point that one could detect a genuine sadness in them every time a truly vicious punch connected, though this subtle eye-misting and display of empathy would, ironically, only be visible to the one closest to the Bawler, that is, the poor bastard of a punching bag getting the stuff.

Demming said he always thought the nickname came from the times Billy's opponents had perished in the ring, prompting the Bawler to rend his satin robe and openly keen.

"Opponents, *plural*?"

"Just telling you the way I heard it, Jay, my man."

Even Alaskan cities "on the rise," like Anchorage and Juneau, retained the rough, Wild West feel of prospectors' towns. The relative scarcity of women, other than military wives and prostitutes, and the starkness and unsentimental brutality of the terrain, especially during the endless night they called winter in these parts, resulted, not surprisingly, in rates of alcoholism and random violence approaching the pandemic. Anchorage, in the late nineteen forties, remained a backwater, the kind of place where men mushed up to the (single) post office or (five) saloons on a dogsled, where beards were grown for warmth and knife fights broke out over gambling disputes involving shotgun shells used as poker chips, where it was not socially frowned upon if one failed to remove one's enormous fur hat indoors, even during a meal, and where the only problem people had with pissing outdoors was that it made the streets slightly muddier if it happened to be warm enough for the mud to unfreeze. (On such rare days, people were generally happy enough about the warmth to forget about the mud.) Jay liked it here all right. He'd grown used to the army work and didn't have anything in particular to rush back home to. Having enlisted at such a young age, he had, in every measurable aspect, become a man in the service, had in fact never experienced adult life on the outside, to such a degree that the civilian world had come to seem the scary and alien one. The sirring, the order, the necessary skirting of both? He *got* all of that.

The venue stank of fish, which was not surprising. Though perhaps the sharp, rotten way the smell lingered could be fairly remarked upon. A pair of promoters had come up with the idea of townie versus soldier, the animosity on both sides thrillingly mutual (and most thrilling of all for the promoters, riled crowds generally making for heavier betting). When pulled aside by his sergeant, Jay agreed to fight almost immediately, because why not? It felt flattering to be asked to represent the base, and he was still young enough to be titillated by the prospect of a larger stage. Then, at some point, he began to notice the looks. They could come at any moment: he might be backing up a forklift, or sliding his tray along the shiny rails of the mess hall buffet line, when he'd catch one of the white soldiers sizing him up. He assumed, at first, the glares came loaded with bitterness, thanks to his being chosen to fight the Irishman in the big bout. Soon, however, he realized they weren't hostile but rather admiring. In every other fight Jay had witnessed at the base in which the opponents had been members of different races, the crowd would likewise segregate itself, the whites violently cheering on their own and the same for the Negroes. Here, though, it seemed as if tribal loyalty to warrior class would trump tribal loyalty to race. The white soldiers, it turned out, hated townies more than black folks, at least in this specific instance of jeopardized military pride.

The night before the fight, at the colored bar in town, Jay took a last sip from a tumbler of whiskey and soda. The other patrons simultaneously fought to buy him drinks and fussed over how he shouldn't get too sauced. For a moment, looking down into his glass of bourbon, the ice cubes slipped to the side, whisking away the distorted, fun-house shapes they produced, and he could see past them, through the bottom of the tumbler to his own left hand resting on the surface below, the Alaskan pine bartop looking through the glass like a murky view of the bed of a lake. And there was his hand—submerged.

What else was there? No cinema. No community theater. No opera house. Occasional live music at Gib's (hillbilly pickers) or the Yukon Palace (bawdy jump blues.) Churches were storefronts, makeshift, often one-offs led by itinerant preachers. Everyone had a second skin of long woolen underwear, typically red, with a classic two-button ass-flap, designed with outhouse trips in mind. For blacks there turned out to be little practical difference between the army and the air force, despite rumors that circulated after the war with regard to the latter treating Negro soldiers with more respect. At Elmendorf in 1949, notwithstanding Truman's recent executive order desegregating all branches of the military, black soldiers continued to work strictly in the capacity of support staff: primarily transport and construction, though men with more specific skills might land jobs as, say, mechanics.

Black servicemen so inclined could frequent a segregated whorehouse stocked with professionals from New Orleans and Kansas City. Bored to tears when not working, the women spent their days lolling in front of the radio, baking pies for a successful pastry side-business, and complaining about the cold. As far as true communal entertainments went, though, the bimonthly Saturday evening boxing matches met with no serious rival. The doors opened at three. Most of the men showed up drunk. Normally, it would be close to midnight when the final match began, depending on how many takers stepped through the ropes during the bottom half of the card, a come-one, come-all amateur invitational that found the untrained participants pummeling each other as if a bar brawl had broken out, leaving many of the losers bloodied wrecks in need of a bone doctor. By the main event, the audience would be properly frothed, a single suspicious dive away from making a bum's rush for the ring themselves. The boxing promoters, the DeMaria brothers, reputedly sent up from Philly by their bosses as a punishment for a botched bribery, staged cards in Juneau, Fairbanks, Nome, a handful of other outposts, and had become organized enough to have a roster of Alaskan champions in various weight divisions.

One of the white privates (Jay couldn't tell you many of their names, so little day-to-day interaction took place) pulled him aside and passed him a lucky tooth, a little incisor once belonging to a kid, tiny as a bean. The white boy said he'd carried it through the war and come out unscratched. He'd kept it in a red ring box with gray felt lining. Jay had been so surprised by the gift, he failed to ask whose tooth, and why, exactly, it was supposed to be so lucky. Others gave him slight words of inspiration or advice, sounding almost affectionate. *You need to keep that big head protected, Cornbread.* Others still, unable to help mixing their encouragement with looks of menace, ended up coming across as vaguely threatening, the clear implication being we'll fuck you up worse than McCann if you blow this for our team, blackie.

Trick is to get yourself mad. Think about that time he raped your mama.

The match went for eight rounds. Demming said until society ended prejudice, blacks would always be superior boxers because getting to whip the ass of a white man with full sanction of the state constituted a very special occasion.

Jay wasn't so sure. It struck him more like a disadvantage, having been trained his entire life to avoid whites, keep out of trouble, and now, suddenly, being encouraged to pummel one? It didn't feel natural, more like a possible trap.

The night of the fight, they'd put the base on high alert. Apparently, the generals had it on good authority: the Russians were coming.

The match itself, well, there's not much to say. The blow-by-blow would sound like any other fight. Some rough stuff on both sides; advantages, openings, retreats. Jay remembered, most vividly, the moment he'd noticed all of the white soldiers cheering him on, which might have felt like an accomplishment but ended up being curiously enervating. He found himself wanting to step into punches, to allow his body to absorb hit after hit, to somehow goad the opposite response from them. He wanted to lie down in the center of the ring and wait for those cheers to turn to boos, curses, epithets, to let the words flow over him like warm, familiar bathwater. Give the crowd what they think they don't want and simultaneously what deep down they actually do.

When the ref raised Jay's gloved fist—this would remain his other primary recollection of the fight—he licked his upper lip and could taste the blood.

CHAPTER SIX

Atlantic City

His Indian mother seemed well. Frailer, of course. Uncharacteristically eager to please. *Got you some apricot juice, I know how much you love it.* He hadn't thought about apricot juice in years. His Indian father died in '48. Heart attack. Both sisters married, still living in the old neighborhood. One of the husbands, a butcher, a good man, insisted on taking Jay out on the town for a proper carousal. The other husband, a clerk at a law firm, claimed exhaustion, but Jay suspected he might be prejudiced.

The butcher had spent the war in France and North Africa, then returned home and bought into the family business. Jay worried his beer coaster, half listening to stories in which the punch line involved boning out sides of beef the wrong way. He told the butcher it felt strange, drinking in a civilian joint. "More females, I'd imagine," the butcher remarked, nodding suggestively at a pair giggling near the jukebox, their dresses holding on to their shapes. One of them used the nickel squeezed between her fingers as a marker, dragging it slowly down the list of records, pausing, pensively tapping the glass with a rounded edge, moving on.

Jay tried to admire the view but felt benumbed. He'd left the country as a boy, come back something else. Claiming manhood, though, he remained ambivalent about that.

The butcher said one of the trickiest things he'd had to learn, professionally, was how to pick out a counterfeit cut of meat. A side of supreme beef, say, that could pass for prime. "So you'll only be paying supreme price, but then can turn around and sell it to the customer as prime," he explained.

"Evil, man," Jay said, his tone flat enough to sound like admiration.

Later that night, in his childhood bedroom, all of the expected emotions were there, keeping him flattened to his mattress. How small everything felt. How all of his moving had failed to halt time, certainly for his mother and sisters. How even one's own metamorphoses read as brazen, back among the familiar. Who could resist comparing their height with the notches on the wall? Those lines Daddy drew.

He hadn't wanted to stay at the bar. He felt like a bad undercover agent, self-conscious, clumsy. Even his voice sounded inappropriately modulated for civilian life, or so he thought. He kept hearing the words *excuse me* come out of his mouth, then caught himself wincing. The butcher, after urging him to chat up the girls, had picked up on Jay's shyness and gently let the matter drop, steering the conversation in the direction of sports, local job opportunities.

Jay pictured himself an apprentice butcher. Bandages mummifying every finger, both hands.

During supper, his sister had said, "Tell us something about your time in the service." All Jay could come up with was how, in Korea, he'd learned to eat with chopsticks.

Jay spent time in Philadelphia after that. Later, Washington, D.C., his birth mother's hometown. Neither city compelled him to stay put. Then, summer of '51, passing through New Jersey with no clear destination in mind, he stopped for lunch in Atlantic City. Three weeks later, he hadn't left.

He could not exactly point to why. He had no local ties, no family there, nor serious acquaintances, and the place remained intensely segregated at the time. You had to cross Atlantic Avenue to get to the black neighborhood, and blacks had their own beach. Whites called it Chicken Bone Beach. Claimed the blacks littered the sand. Generally speaking, the police preferred not to see colored faces on the boardwalk.

Of course, he loved the black nightclub district, centered on North Kentucky Avenue and known locally as "the Curb." Club Harlem offered a full floor show, featuring comics, chorus girls, and a house band (the Crazy Chris Columbo Combo, led by Columbo, a drummer who'd gigged with Fletcher Henderson), and drew all of the top performers of the day: Duke Ellington, Count Basie, Louis Jordan, the Mills Brothers. Jay frequented the bars and clubs nightly, usually hitting one or more of the smaller spots—Gracie's Little Belmont, Paradise, the Wonder Garden, Paddock International Bar—before heading over to Club Harlem's "breakfast show," which got started around six in the morning and attracted players from the other clubs around town, who'd be invited onstage by the featured act for this fourth and final set.

By this point Jay had overcome his awkwardness around women. His need to allude to some form of vaguely joblike aspiration had led him to begin describing himself as a musician. To some chicks he declared himself a pianist, a singer to others; the lie closer to half of a truth, as he'd never quit on his childhood dream of opera fame. Even if, true, he'd done zilch to pursue it. Sometimes he wondered if he preferred the potential energy of fantasy.

Nights he found himself in a particular mood, Jay would excuse himself from whatever chorus girl or cocktail waitress he happened to be making time with and steal out to the boardwalk, alone. Friends warned him about the danger of this habit. But the cops never bothered him. Perhaps it was the hour. Perhaps, despite his size, he looked unassuming enough, shambling stiffly in his one good suit.

He took such a walk on the night he met Lloyd "Tiny" Grimes, the guitarist and bandleader. A girlfriend had hipped him to a potential job opening, Tiny apparently looking to hire a personal valet and chauffeur at thirty bucks a week. Jay swung by the Winter Garden to catch his show, grabbing a table near the back of the room with a different girl, Georgia, herself a singer. Onstage, Tiny's latest outfit, a quintet called the Rocking Highlanders, had just started playing "Saint Louis Blues." For a black rhythm-and-blues group, the Highlanders had stumbled onto a very peculiar gimmick: they dressed like Scotsmen, wearing kilts, brogues, tam-o'-shanters, knee-length highlander socks, frilly white shirts cut in the billowing "Jacobite style," and piper's jackets. The idea had supposedly come to Grimes after the band worked up a swing version of "Loch Lomond."

When Jay told his date about the possible gig, she whispered, "You think he's going to make you wear some kind of Scottish motorist's outfit?" Jay pulled an exaggerated scowl. But the prospect of public humiliation did concern him, badly as he craved entrée into the show world. Tight as the number sounded, he was having trouble getting past the band's clownish shtick. Grimes, a balding man with a broad mouth and crooked teeth, not one of those Tinys who'd earned his nickname ironically, grinned at the crowd. His kilt seemed to billow in mock-time with the notes he plucked from his four-string.

"Awfully corny," Jay murmured.

His date snorted. "Who the hell are you? He's the real

deal, brother. That man used to be in a trio with Art Tatum, our greatest living pianist. He's cut sides with Charlie Parker, our greatest living horn player. He's backed up Billie Holiday, our greatest living singer. What the fuck's on your c.v., exactly, other than a clean driver's license?"

Jay lacked a great retort for all of that.

His uniform ended up being a variation on the standard chauffeur's livery: dark suit, short-brimmed driving cap, leather gloves. Tiny decided the kilts would be reserved for the band.

Tiny preferred to ride in the passenger seat of the Cadillac while Jay shuttled him to gigs, liquor stores, guitar shops, a Scottish haberdashery in Philadelphia's Little Edinburgh. The occasional whimsical demand—a midnight run, say, to his favorite spaghetti joint in Harlem. Three hours each way from A.C. and the place turned out to be a diner.

Lengthier hauls, Tiny would fall into extended periods of silence. Jay didn't mind, unless Tiny tuned the radio to a religious station, an odd habit for a man who never otherwise discussed church-going or holy rolling of any sort. The stations played gospel music, recordings of sermons. One had a Bible call-in show.

Evening, Pastor. I have a question. Is it true that Jesus stripped the Devil of his powers? And if so—

"That through death, He might destroy the one who has the power of death, that is, the Devil." Hebrews. Forgive me for interrupting, young man, but I have heard your question before. And I suspect you also want to know if this means the Devil no longer has any powers over the wicked and the unbelievers? I am

here to tell you NO, sir, it does NOT. Now would you care to guess why?

Uh . . . 'Cause we ain't Jesus?

Amen, brother.

Tiny never commented on the Bible talk. On occasion, Jay caught his head tilted all the way back, the brimless pulp of his tam pulled down near the tip of his nose.

As Jay grew comfortable around the older man, he felt emboldened to coax forth stories. Bird? Nice guy, friendly. He used to show up at Tondaleyo's on Fifty-Second Street to jam with Tiny's trio. Matter of fact, Tiny'd been the one who first took him into a recording studio, back when he was cutting sides for Savoy Records. Herman Lubinsky, the label owner, had balked at paying for an extra musician when Tiny brought Parker along to the sessions. Six months later, after Bird had taken flight, Lubinsky had no problem switching around the billing on the record. Then it became "Charlie Parker, feat. the Tiny Grimes Trio."

I harbor no will. Man had a business.

Slam Stewart? Big fellow. Slam's thing was, while he played the bass, he hummed along, but an octave lower. Cute trick. They twinned up after Slim Gaillard, the jive vocalist, other half of Slim and Slam, got drafted. Tiny and Slam had a regular gig together out in California, at Lovejoy's Chicken Shack on Central Avenue. That's how they met Art Tatum.

Now Tatum, he had a twelve-key span, and he would constantly be working a filbert nut through his fingers. Insisted it kept them nimble. He was also going blind by that point. He'd always played solo, but one of his managers had convinced him to try doing his thing with a couple of real showpeople like Slam and Tiny, maybe broaden his appeal.

Up to Art? He'd of stuck to after-hours joints. He loved staying up all night, getting into cutting contests with other dudes.

One night, Slam looked at Art bothering his nut and said, "You know what the white boys back in Boston used to call filberts? 'Nigger toes.'"

Art grunted, then said, "I had a buddy who lost his toes. Fingers, too. His blood went septic, so the doctor took 'em off. Left him with paddles and loaves."

Slam said, "Septic, huh?" Then he broke into a little tune.

> I told her I'd love to oblige,
> 'Cept, Sis,
> Doc took my fingers away.

Funny, Jay thought, the things people remembered.

During intermissions, Tiny said, he would retreat to the basement and practice whatever song they'd been playing, trying to catch up with the fellows as best he could. He never understood why in the world those two kept him around. He knew he was the weakest thing in there. The low man on the Tatum pole, as he liked to joke. He said Art and Slam both had perfect pitch, so you could hit on a glass and they'd tell you what note it was. Or what notes it was between. And because Slam had that perfect ear, Tatum couldn't lose him.

Me, he could lose.

He said, once? Billie Holiday had a cold, or claimed to, most likely dope-sickness, and the two of them left the studio and walked over to a chop suey joint. She got hot and sour soup to clear her sinuses, but only ate two bites. Ace tipper, though.

* * *

That first night at the Wonder Garden, Jay made his way backstage after the Highlanders wrapped their final set. The band hadn't changed out of their costumes yet. As Jay sought out Tiny's dressing room, he caught a glimpse of the men playing cards, drinking, and smoking, their shirts now loosened for comfort, shoes and hats discarded, but the kilts still hanging off them like any other uniform at day's end. It reminded him of the workers he'd seen on subway trains, just off their shifts, waiters in tuxedoes, liveried bellhops, grease monkeys in their zippered coveralls; that contrast between the implied servitude of appointed dress and the freedom to smoke a cigarette, slump all the way back on your bench, read a book, flirt audaciously with the nurse all in white. Only the soldier can walk about in full uniform, far from his place of duty, and not appear absurd, Jay thought.

Tiny himself sat alone in his dressing room, still crabbed over his guitar, looking as if he'd be ready to absorb the thing into his body. The kilt's wrinkled tartan clung rather tightly to his legs, like a second skin inexplicably unshed.

After some initial chitchat about the job, Tiny asked if Jay played.

Jay cleared his throat and said, "Used to. Piano. Fooled around with a horn some while I was doing my time in the service. Really singing was always what I'd hoped to work up to."

Tiny didn't reply, just watched Jay as if he, Tiny, were the one being patient.

Finally he said, "No piano, as you can see."

* * *

The interview hadn't lasted long, but by the time Jay headed out into the night, it was close to five in the morning. At this hour, the boardwalk always felt, to Jay, like a ledge. He loved staring out at the ocean, its glowering unlit presence looming from below. The sea's proximity made the rest of the town feel like a cheap prop-set, like one of those fake bookmaker's joints or stock brokerages set up by a team of guys pulling a long con.

Eminently portative, this world.

They added a piano, eventually, but by that point, Jay had mostly lost interest in playing such jazz-inflected rhythm-and-blues. It no longer felt natural to him. He preferred the new sound he'd been hearing since he came home from the war.

Grimes did eventually allow his young protégé to sing on a couple of tracks.

CHAPTER SEVEN

Scream Blacula Scream

They met one night at WINS in midtown Manhattan. Stan Pat, Jay's manager, had arranged the visit. Alan Freed wore a shirt and tie while broadcasting, though typically he removed his jacket and draped it over the back of his chair. On this particular night he had also rolled up his shirtsleeves. Jay thought he looked like a banker preparing to wash the dishes.

A sign at the console flashed ON AIR. Freed, his skull forcepped with a pair of outsized headphones, pulled the microphone to his face and said, "I'm back with an ax, little girls. Don't make me use it to get in there. I'd hate to split a perfectly good door. You know how much your daddy paid to buy that door? It came with the house, I'm sure, so even he'd probably be hard-pressed to make a reasonable estimate. But I'll tell you one thing, and you can take this to the World Bank: he won't be pleased with my handiwork."

Freed believed performers often forgot the importance of making an entrance. "I'm telling you, a *casket*," he said to Jay, off the air. Stan nodded like he'd been the one advocating for this all along. Freed went on, "Remember, when an audience finally fixes their eyes on a guy they've been hearing on the radio, it is a powerful experience for all parties concerned. But you control that first impression. And what could be more memorable?"

Jay said, "Than being dead?"

Freed, not catching the skepticism, nearly shouted, "And then alive!"

There was a signal from the control booth. Freed held up a finger, replaced his headphones, and began nodding along with the end of the tune, finally speaking into the microphone, "That was so nice, I'm-a do it twiiiiice . . . "

The same record began playing again.

The day after their meeting with Freed, Stan and Jay visited a funeral parlor in Gowanus.

The coffins were arranged by price, in subsets of color. Mr. Browning, the funeral director, pointed out the key features of various models: finer grains of wood, the ornate gilding lavished upon more baroque grips and handles.

Jay, lagging behind, ran a finger along the center of a mahogany lid polished to an oily sheen. Leaning forward at the waist, he held his nose inches from the casket and inhaled deeply.

Looked roomy enough.

"How well ventilated are these things?" Jay called out.

Browning, misunderstanding, assured him they were airtight.

They'd have to drill some holes in the head-end. Easily done.

Jay cracked one of the fancier models. The deep red lining of the inside of the box brought to mind a dissected animal. Guts.

He stroked the lining with the back of his hand, the way he would a baby's cheek or a woman's. Something soft, caught asleep.

"Solid," he said.

He allowed the lid to drop. It made a clattering sound as it fell shut.

"I think we're probably in the market for something a bit simpler," Stan murmured, flipping through a catalog provided by Browning. On the page on which he'd paused, the depicted coffin, a rich oak, had been lit to resemble a perfect cut of steak.

"Certainly," Browning said. "We accommodate the entire range."

"Father was a very pious man. He would have considered expenses like these—"

"This is true," Jay interrupted. "But we also want Daddy to be comfortable."

"No one is talking about sacrificing comfort. I just think we would be respecting his wishes by finding a happy *medium* and—"

"Happy? You going to be in there? Or him?"

"There's always cremation."

"He wouldn't have wanted that."

"Toss the old scoundrel in the oven. Might be kind of satisfying."

"Poor old Dad. I'm sorry you had one really bad, son."

"Remember what Mother said: 'Money is tight, boys.'"

"That greedy cow. Always grabbing up fifteen percent of Father's hard-earned income. Spending it on Cuban rum, dog races."

"Mr. Browning, I hope you'll forgive our banter. It's our way of grieving."

Clearing his throat, Browning asked, "Do you have a pastor? To say a few words?"

"He wasn't a religious man."

"Catering?"

"All set."

"Flowers?"

"What do you think, brother? Too much?"

"Might be distracting to the audience."

"He means the mourners."

"Of course. And also too feminine."

"There is that."

"I ain't Little Richard."

"You mean the deceased."

"Daddy was not Little Richard."

"He means the rhythm-and-blues singer. 'Wap-ba-ba-loo-ba'? An inside joke. Daddy would go around saying, 'Who do you think you're talking to, Little Richard?'"

"Not that Daddy listened to rhythm-and-blues music."

"He'd just heard the name and found it amusing."

"He thought it sounded like a slang term for a tiny—you know."

"He was a stupid, stupid man."

"Amused by the vulgar."

"I'll miss the old bastard."

Browning asked when the body would be arriving.

Stan Pat explained that they would be taking the coffin with them.

"Private viewing," Jay said.

"But someone must prepare the body!"

"Mother."

"She insists."

The undertaker said this was highly unusual. He repeated this statement when he saw the van in which the pair proposed to load the coffin.

"We'll need a receipt," Stan said.

On the way out, they passed a child-sized coffin. It might have been luggage.

* * *

Stan came upon Jay, backstage, a couple of nights into the tour, staring at the open-lidded coffin. Planted there with his fingers massaging his hips, he looked like a man confronted with a botched surprise. The piñata splits, revealing nothing but torn paper flesh. The cake erupts but conceals no woman; it is just a cake-shaped box. Stan clapped him on the shoulder, said something like, "You ready, Houdini?" Jay, clearly not up for a lark; Stan ascribed the mood to preshow jitters.

The pressures of the Freed-promoted package jubilees (also called "revues," "dances," and "coronation balls") were intense for the performers, the marquees packed with dozens of acts, each playing for approximately seven minutes up to eight times a day, the same two-three songs, again and over again, for an audience of hysterical children. The first show typically began around noon, with hopped-up teenagers ushered into whatever palatial theater Freed had booked. It was teenagers all day, teenagers by the thousands, white kids and black kids, sometimes (depending on the city) directed to separate entrances, with certain venues restricting the whites to balcony seating while the Negroes danced in front of the stage.

Camaraderie, sure, but also competition. The vocal groups (the Drifters, the Spaniels, the Clovers, the Moonglows) stuck together, as far as Stan could tell, while straight rhythm-and-blues acts who'd come out of the clubs tended to resent the younger rock and rollers as hacks and degenerates who had lucked into a passing fad. Speaking of, Little Frankie Lymon, the pipsqueak delinquent, already changed into his letter jacket and pressed slacks, sidled up next to them. His eyes looked bloodshot, though his head barely reached Jay's rib-cage.

"Spooky, man," he muttered at the casket, sounding serious, and then offered Jay a toke from his funny cigarette. Jay declined, absently waggling his own flask of bourbon, though in truth he barely seemed to register the boy, his thoughts elsewhere.

When he finally climbed inside, he reminded Stan of an old Russian at the *banya* lowering himself into a tub of icy water. Arms rigid, supporting his weight from behind. Bracing himself for the heart-stopping plunge.

Jay would be the first to admit, he *had* been gripped by a queer mood. The initial rehearsal went off well, but each subsequent tour in the casket proved more difficult, such that he began to wonder if he might be afflicted with some latent form of claustrophobia. In the handful of moments he spent lying there in the blackness, his costume damply clutching at his skin, the simple act of breathing shifted to the forefront of his consciousness, and he found himself gulping down the air, panicked and greedy. When the band finally hit its cue, signaling Jay to batter open the lid and make his exit, he felt like a drowning man breaking the surface of the ocean.

Between sets, he did his best to play it cool. Razzing the other musicians, talking shop: unpaid royalties, sharks at the label, wives versus jailbait, man that horn on so-and-so's killer new side. When it came time to reenter the casket, he made an effort to disguise his discomfort, announcing, "My chariot awaits," or cracking wise about the hazards of self-pleasure in tightly enclosed spaces. The pallbearers, after gingerly fold-ing over the edges of his cape, looked down expectantly, hold-ing out for a nod, which Jay attempted to infuse with a professional impatience. *Get on with it, man! We got a show to do.*

The tidal crawl of the lid's shadow passed across his face, the lid itself trailing by seconds. Involuntarily, Jay steeled himself, squeezing his eyes shut just before the final darkness.

Jay came to fix his dread more accurately. He realized it had less to do with the enclosed space, per se, than with the coffin itself. Which surprised him; he'd never considered himself especially superstitious. True, he'd held a morbid disposition for as long as he could remember, even as a boy. But Jay never would have guessed such an unsubtle memento mori as a source of his unhinging. A skull in a fruit bowl had a milder allegorical touch. If anything, he'd assumed joking about his fear, burlesquing it, might act as a sort of salve, just as his costume burlesqued uncomfortable questions about race, burlesqued his very blackness, in fact, or rather his white audience's *perception of* said blackness, with Jay using the cape, the bones, the fetish objects, what Stan called his "ooga-booga boogie-woogie," to nod at the tension inherent in black men performing sexually charged music for white teenagers. Jay wanted to give his paler fans something to feast their eyes and glut their souls upon. Likewise, facing death in such a ridiculous way, with a coffin as a prop in a glorified nightclub act, had felt like an inoculation, a means of transforming his most elemental fear into the set-up of a punch line. Now, though, he wondered if the role, and all that came with it, might be infecting his mind; if, like a character out of Poe, he'd allowed a single object to take on such symbolic weight, it threatened to drive him mad.

As with the narrator of "The Premature Burial," Jay's "fancy grew charnel." Though, to be fair, the morbid obsessions of Poe's hero circled a specific, highly implausible scenario: a cataleptic, the character becomes convinced he will lapse into a trance and awaken sealed in a tomb. Jay had no such medical externalities driving his neurosis. He'd simply come to believe that he would die inside that coffin, as if a truth had been revealed to him.

All of which resulted in a marked improvement in his performances. Every time the lid of that casket launched into space, Jay experienced the fleeting joy of a condemned man granted a reprieve, unleashing howls unlike any heretofore mustered. Freed pulled him aside after a show in Philly, told him Jerry Lee Lewis, the hillbilly piano player, had asked if he should consider writing spookier tunes, maybe throw on a turban, or a mad professor's lab coat.

His behavior grew more eccentric as the tour headed south and his alcohol intake rose accordingly. Stan knew Jay had toured below the Mason-Dixon line before, with Fats Domino and others, but he began to worry the Jim Crow gigs might be pushing him over the edge. He was starting to freak out the kids, Stan could see it in their eyes, even from the wings: a certain self-protective flinching, pegged to his entrance, or rather exit, from the coffin, Jay's own eyes no longer betraying any trace of humor, never seeming to wink along with the joke. He'd begun sleeping in his burial suit, which took on a musty, threadbare authenticity.

When they arrived in Atlanta, local authorities had drawn a rope down the central aisle of that night's theater, marking a clear visual indicator of the rules of the house. Coloreds would only be allowed to sit on the right side of the rope, whites on the left.

"Surprising," Stan whispered, surveying the floor with Jay for the first time, "the promoters' failure to secure a slightly more aesthetically pleasing line of demarcation. A long sash, perhaps, or even a clothesline garlanded with bunting or tinsel."

Jay nodded, tipping his flask. The ugly hemp rope, waist high and tied to a pair of squat metal posts that normally held up velvet cords, looked more appropriate for lashing a tarp over a pile of shipping containers.

"Though in a pinch," he said, "easily segmentable for multiple lynchings."

Stan chuckled nervously. "I understand, this means of division is chosen to send a message: *We ain't foolin'*. Still, a token respect for the local architecture would have been nice, no? This theater deserves a less severe touch."

Jay, only half listening, did not even crack a smile. Stan sighed and looked away, suddenly taking in the entirety of the Moorish-style movie palace, probably built in the twenties: gilded rococo moldings, maroon seat cushions, faux lanterns throwing off smoky mood lighting, carpet befitting a sultan's bedchamber. That rope slashing its belly like a long white scar.

"You okay, pal?" he asked softly, not looking back at his friend. "You haven't seemed yourself lately." There was no response. Stan whispered, "Don't let these crackers get you down."

In Macon, another theater, the lid of the casket failed to open. The band members exchanged nervous glances, imperceptible to the audience. *We hit the cue, right?*

Smoking a cigarette on a catwalk above the stage, Elsbeary Hobbs, the bass singer from the Drifters, peered curiously onto the scene. The band, vamping around its basket, coaxed forth no snake. Even the kids seemed to be picking up on the problem, their expectant grins beginning to fade.

Suddenly, Hobbs noticed a movement in the shadows. It was Jay Hawkins.

"Hey, look, it's Sir Graves Ghastly," Hobbs said, pleasantly enough. "Only, ain't you supposed to be down there?"

Jay muttered something affirmative sounding that Hobbs couldn't quite make out. "Hey, that's cool, man," Hobbs said, palms raised. "I don't rat." The men had barely spoken on the tour, but Hawkins' act cracked him up, or had, before it started turning weird. Tonight, he reeked of booze.

From above, the coffin looked like a raft. A piece of furniture. Hobbs, chuckling, said, "Reminds me of a painting." He meant the crowd, the way the stage lights threw shadows onto those kids' dopey faces. Also, their uncanny stillness. He had a word, on the tip of his tongue. *Diptych*, he finally said. An art-fancying Sunday school teacher from his childhood, Hobbs explained, had taken his class up to the Cloisters and devoted an entire lesson to the early days of the Christian church, when painters split certain panels right down the middle, into "diptychs of the living" and "diptychs of the dead," each side depicting various holy figures: bishops, martyrs, popes. The Macon theater had no rope, but as in Atlanta, the room had been divided into black kids and white ones.

Stan had shuffled onto the stage, looking like he was attempting his own awkward version of a Chuck Berry duck walk. Approaching the coffin, he cracked the lid enough to peep inside, then dropped it almost immediately, as if his fingers had flecked the hot edge of a frying pan. In retreat, he made frantic gestures toward the wings, and moments later, the Cadillacs, a five-man group from Harlem, jogged into the spotlight to form a slightly obscuring phalanx at the front of the casket. Hawkins' resourceful band somehow pulled out a raggedy, still impressive transition into the Caddys' big hit, "Speedoo." No one moved the coffin, which forced the doo-woppers to adjust their choreography accordingly.

Jay had been enjoying the kids staring at the coffin. He thought of a title for Hobbs' painting: *Teenyboppers Forced to Contemplate Their Own Mortality*. He didn't share the title with Hobbs. Just then, a girl from the white half of the painting glanced into the rafters, her eyes meeting Jay's. She looked so innocent. For the first time in days, the beginning of a smirk crept across Jay's face.

The crowd had just resumed bopping its collective head, in a way that made both sides of the diptych almost shimmer, when the girl loosed a piercing scream. The band abruptly halted the number, and the Cadillacs froze, midshimmy. Even Hobbs took a few steps back, looking like a man who'd just realized he might be sharing a cigarette with an escaped murderer.

Jay, for his part, betrayed little surprise. The girl's reaction had been something out of an old horror movie, sticking him with the Karloff role: a guileless monster, not yet aware of his own hideousness, believing he could win friends with freshly plucked flowers.

And so, staring out at the upturned faces, he did the only thing he could do, at least in his mind. He lifted his arms, allowing his cape to fall open and spread into wings, and then, calmly, he stepped over the railing.

Didn't she know, this was a different picture altogether? He wasn't interested in drowning anybody.

CHAPTER EIGHT

Because You're Mine

Placing his hand on the small of Bettina's back, Jay leaned forward and whispered, "Why don't you come upstairs? The emperor needs a male heir."

A drink in his face. Later, though, after they were properly introduced, she became friendlier and eventually did visit his hotel room.

For Charlotte, oranges were "aranges," bad guys always "that louse," movies "pickchas."

A very New York girl.

"Have I ever told you the story of Henry?" Jay would periodically ask his audience, holding the skull-topped staff aloft. The story, according to the man who'd sold Jay the skull, went like this: Henry had once been a monk, leading a pious and ascetic life of contemplation, until one day, the devil appeared before him. The monk had been having trouble rousing himself for his morning prayers, and the horned one came bearing "a humble peace offering," a rooster. Of course, Henry greeted the gesture with suspicion, considering its source, but upon further reflection, he could see no potential for sin in such a minor easement of his daily rituals. And so he accepted the bird, and sure enough, in the weeks that followed, its crowing made the chore of waking at dawn an immeasurably simpler one—to such a degree that, when the rooster became listless and sickly, and eventually stopped eating altogether, the monk found himself equally distraught.

At which point, the devil reappeared. "Your rooster is lonely," he informed Henry. The cure required no special veterinary skills, merely the purchase of a hen to keep the old bird company. Henry stiffened at the prospect of further cluttering his spare existence. But he'd also come to depend on the rooster, and part of him believed the addition of a hen could actually be a Christian act of charity. So, once more, against his better judgment, he took the devil's advice. As promised, the presence of the hen swiftly alleviated the rooster's dyspepsia. And yet as the birds, frolicking in the yard, allowed nature to take its course, the monk found himself taking what some might describe as an unhealthy level of interest in the devilish cure. Embers he'd thought long extinguished began to smolder once more!

A week later, crazed by lust, Henry sinned with the daughter of a local nobleman. When the girl threatened to tell her parents, he strangled her to death and hid her body in a copse on the manor grounds.

The girl's murder was soon discovered; Henry, arrested, tried, and sentenced to die.

On the day of his execution, after the hangman had slipped a noose around his neck—at this point in the story, Jay would grip the top end of his staff, just below the skull's chin, with an especial tightness—the local magistrate asked Henry if he had any last words. The monk turned to face the crowd that had gathered to witness his ultimate punishment. He paused for a moment, considering what he might say. Then, finally, he cried out: "Behold, to what end a cock has brought me!"

After a rimshot from the drummer, the band started playing "Little Demon." Pearl, seated in the front row, had recognized the old tale, having read a version while studying abroad in Bologna. Jay, noticing her smile of recognition, gave her a wink in return.

They had a longer conversation about the devil after the show.

When Phyllis began to sniffle, Jay told her that Chinese barbers, in the nineteenth century, had tools called "eye cleaners"—just a shaft of glass used to tickle the eyeball and coax forth cleansing tears. He'd seen one in a museum in England, years back.

In hindsight, not the best time for such an anecdote.

"You're missing it," Grace said.

He had his back to the water. Rockets, also behind him, exploded in the night sky, strobing the view with fragile constellations. Jay continued to stare at his girl, though.

She held a little plastic flag on a stick, but loosely; it listed from her grip like the pencil of a bored student. The edge of the flag, prodded by spiny blades of grass, crumpled up against itself, red stripes throbbing dully from beneath the overlapping whites.

The other couples all faced the same direction, shoulders touching, hands piled together in one or another's lap. But Jay had settled into his spot on the park lawn and would not be pulled around. Grace looked fondly at him, clearly flattered by the attention. To be chosen over a rare spectacle! Even so, her eyes could not help but drift to the shimmering colored lights bursting on the far side of her suitor's head, which would have looked like manifestations of his overexcited thoughts, had his expression not remained so placid.

He, in turn, stole glances at the sea of upturned faces behind her, all smiling in the glow of the magic like stupefied children. None looked his way. Jay felt moved by the tragic vulnerability of humans, lapsing so easily into states of distracted satiation. Would be so easy to cut every one of their damned throats.

He listened to the distant poppings, which sounded like paper bags filled with air and then burst with fists. Behind Grace and her fellow spectators, a brand-new apartment building loomed on a distant block. Jay could see the fireworks reflected in the windows, only it looked as if the blasts were taking place inside the tower, colored flames silently filling a dark aquarium, the panes glowing with an infernal beauty. A vague memory flashed in Jay's mind, of watching a disaster on television with the volume turned all the way down.

Grace was smiling at him now, directly meeting his gaze. He made silent word-shapes with his mouth. She leaned closer, squinting, the better to read his lips. His eyes flicked over her shoulder one last time. Try as he might, he could not recall the specific catastrophe.

Now he wet the tip of his finger in his mouth, lifted Coral's necklace by the clasp, traced a straight line directly underneath. Blew it dry.

At the restaurant, Letty, who'd mentioned several times how she never touched alcohol, revealed a habit even more unseemly: seizing her glass of water, she filled her mouth completely, forcing her cheeks to distend, and only then did she allow herself to swallow, her throat pulsing like a python's. Jay wondered, though not aloud, *Who taught you to drink this way?*

In all other respects, a very pretty girl. Her father was a state senator.

They met at the Glyptotek Museum in Copenhagen. She'd been wheeling her father through a room filled with Etruscan busts. The ancient faces, intact but for long-crumbled noses, glowered leprously from artfully arranged pedestals. Jay felt like she'd returned his stare, but the problem of the old man seemed potentially insurmountable. He clutched a leather-bound book, most likely a journal of some sort, atop his tartan lap blanket and with his other hand pointed out various sculptural details with a pencil. From across the room, he seemed like an insufferable pedant; the girl covered her mouth and nervously kneaded her cheeks, obviously stifling a yawn. Jay began to move in their direction, weaving between the head-supporting columns with serpentine finesse. Neither father nor daughter possessed especially Scandinavian features, and when he got closer, Jay could hear the old fellow speaking British English. Something about a famous art forger. Jay traced a wide half crescent around the stationary pair and came to a halt directly behind the likeness being lectured upon, though he made sure to lock eyes with another, similarly bearded visage in the corner, giving the girl a partially obstructed view of his back. The shrill, quavering voice of the father carried easily to this new position. Apparently, to falsely age a bust, the first step involved soaking it, for at least a month, in a barrel of vinegar; then . . . Jay casually turned around and met the girl's stare. Ventured a smile, implying empathy with her present lot. The pirouette had been well timed, as the old man, though still speaking, was consulting his own notes. Jay cast a meaningful glance at a passage leading to the next room. The girl leaned forward and, physically pausing the old man's lecture with a hand gently placed across his breast, whispered something in his ear. He scowled, nodding impatiently, and she strode toward the next room, giving Jay a long look as she went.

After a brief interval, Jay followed her. The next room was dominated by urns of various sizes. The girl had continued on to the following room, the museum's famous winter garden, where she stood gazing up at the fronds of a massive palm tree, one of several dozen soaring up in the direction of the ornate central dome. Nearby, children tossed coins into a gaudily appointed fountain, one of them clearly attempting to blind the pool's alabaster centerpiece, a smug naiad. Jay approached the girl, admiring the fit of her skirt. Before he had a chance to speak, she said, "Be succinct. My husband is a jealous lunatic." It took Jay a moment to understand she was talking about the old man. "Oh, so," he said. "Succinct," she said. Her accent, also British, sounded posher than the old man's. "Right," Jay said. "Well, I'm staying in a hotel just off the square." "I'm joking about my husband," she said. "He is my husband. But he's not jealous. In fact, he likes to watch other men have their way with me. Would that make you uncomfortable?" Jay said he expected not.

They went to the couple's hotel instead of Jay's. While the wife paid the taxi driver, the old man asked Jay if he would wheel him into the lobby. Only as they reached the elevator did Jay pick up on the choreography at work, how he'd been meant to play the role of servant.

Upstairs, the husband ended up doing much of the talking, lecturing Jay about jazz, its crude modalities, explaining the wine. Jay sat beside the man's wife on an ornate fainting sofa, where she casually placed her hand on his crotch as the old man droned on. Jay looked forward to fucking her while the husband watched, helplessly, even if this humiliation would actually bring the old man pleasure. At the very least, it would shut him up.

Eventually, the woman said, "You're boring us, Valentine," and abruptly stood up and retreated to the bathroom. Soon they could hear water filling the tub. The husband had resumed his monologue, by this point having turned to giving Jay various investment tips. "Are you coming?" the woman called out after a few moments. Jay stared at the man, gave him a half shrug, and finally said, "Excuse me," before rising to join her.

Later, in the mirror, he caught a glimpse of the husband furiously masturbating from across the other room, the man's penis looking, at this angle, like an enormous extra thumb. His lower jaw, jutting slightly, formed the beginning of an underbite—Jay had noticed this feature earlier in the evening—suggesting, in this new context, a perpetual, gritt-toothed concentration. Though with the penis-thumb, he appeared to be warning Jay about some coming threat with an obscure crotch-level hand signal.

Jay closed his eyes and lowered his forehead to the man's wife's bare stomach, which, counterintuitively, had a cooling effect.

During moments of passion, Vernadette's mouth fell open, and she looked as if she were trying to lift something extremely heavy that simply wouldn't budge.

* * *

This girl Beulah could really drink. Jay had spotted her across a crowded bar, having noticed in particular her habit, when taking a sip of beer, of tilting the bottle sideways, rather than frontally, like a nurse pouring disinfectant into an open wound.

It took him a few moments to understand that in her usage, the word *nervous* meant something closer to "angrily agitated."

"*Now* you're making me nervous!" she shouted at her opponents.

Beulah turned out to be a lady wrestler. Large woman. She wore overalls and pretended to be a pig farmer from Nebraska. Her ring name was Sooey Generous, which Jay found impressive, though later, he learned her manager had come up with it.

For years afterward, he could close his eyes and feel her bosom pushed against his back as she locked his arms into a full Nelson. A drunken, topless demonstration, during which Jay had become aroused, despite the pain emanating from his twisted arms.

In the ring, her tag team partner had been Elvira Snodgrass, the Wrestling Hillbilly.

They began arriving at the Sunset Marquis just after seven, though the invitation said eight. A young white girl holding a clipboard greeted them enthusiastically in the lobby. "Oh, Mr. Hendricks! Welcome!" she said to Marvin Hendricks, who arrived at closer to eight thirty. "How was your flight from . . . Detroit, correct?" She was correct! She also made clear her knowledge of what he did for a living (a staff therapist at a juvenile detention center) and certain family details (two kids), and Marvin got the sense, as she ushered him toward the courtyard pool area where the reunion was taking place, that she had probably also memorized his age and marital status (thirty-seven, divorced), as well as, of course, his ranking among the bastards. According to a password-protected section of the official World Wide Web site, Marvin was the thirteenth male and twenty-fourth overall of Screamin' Jay Hawkins' extramarital offspring.

They'd come from Philadelphia, Paris, Southern California, Juneau, Texas, Tallahassee, Guanajuato, Coney Island. They displayed a multiplicity of ages, body types, complexions, styles of dress. The youngest, a seven-year-old from Bowling Green, Kentucky, was accompanied by an ever-watchful mother; the oldest, a fifty-three-year-old surgeon practicing in Toronto, brought his own teenage daughter, a first-year art history major at McGill who wanted to take a tour of the new Getty Center and see the Hollywood Walk of Fame. One of the brothers had actually dressed like Jay: cape, skull-staff, bone through his nose, the works. Though maybe he wasn't actually a brother, but just some guy hired by the organizers of the event.

They'd shown up for a variety of reasons. Some, like Janessa, an airline pilot based out of Minneapolis, had known their father's identity from an early age. For others, the revelation had come more recently and been received as a seismic shift. Marvin, for example, whose mother, an eleventh-grade English teacher, private and bookish, had always refused to say much about his biological father, except that she hadn't known him, really, beyond that one-night stand; he'd come through Detroit while on military leave, died in Vietnam. But something one of Marvin's uncles had said, a crack one Christmas Eve, had always made him suspect the Vietnam story was bullshit. Marvin read his uncle's hint as implying his true father had been a musician of some reknown, a genetic fantasy Marvin found both flattering and certainly more fun to secretly speculate upon. Had Otis Redding or Miles Davis, gigging in Detroit one wintry eve in 1965, found themselves smitten by the young cocktail waitress at Baker's Keyboard Lounge? Or perhaps, it being Detroit after all, one of the Temptations, or even—would his mother have provided such a throbbing neon clue?—Marvin Gaye himself?

She finally confessed in the most awkward way possible, at one of their regular Wednesday dinners. As Marvin sat down at the table, he noticed a newspaper clipping, neatly folded and tucked beneath his napkin—a short article about how the late musician responsible for "I Put a Spell on You," a song Marvin only knew from the Nina Simone version, had fathered scores of illegitimate children, all of whom had been invited to attend a "family reunion" in Los Angeles, providing they brought some manner of proof and were willing to sign a release form for a planned documentary.

"Marvin Gaye!" his mother exclaimed when he revealed

his own long-harbored notions. "But you know you were named after your grandfather's best friend Marvin Sturgis!"

Marvin had known that, of course, but had convinced himself Sturgis must be a convenient cover story.

Screamin' Jay Hawkins, though! A number of the children—not only Marvin—found this news difficult to process. They went out to record stores (some of them for the first time in years), picked up greatest-hits CDs, and listened to their father's strange, jokey tunes while scrutinizing liner-note photographs for some trace of a familial resemblance and poring over the details of the old man's ridiculous, unbelievable life. They'd all come to the reunion bearing varying degrees of skepticism. Some of them wondered if the organizers of the event hoped to turn their group meeting into a kind of freakshow. Others held vague hopes of a surprise monetary reward, some manner of deathbed amends ordered by their absent father, and they came picturing dozens of gathered heirs seated in folding chairs beneath a massive tent as a lawyer solemnly read from the revised will. Most of them hoped to find, to a greater or lesser degree, some trace of themselves—something that had existed out in the world for these many years, scattered, but a true part of them, something no one could deny as real.

Over the course of the evening, Marvin met a catalog photographer, a dogcatcher, a meteorologist, an Asian studies professor, a retired professional soccer coach, a coder at Netscape, a janitor, a twenty-six-year-old mother of five from the Bay Area, a gay single dad from Wichita. They'd all missed having a biological father around, even though some had stepdads or other surrogates (in Marvin's case, his mother's two older brothers). They shared such intimacies delicately at first. A few of them flirted, in spite of the unspoken taboo. Marvin had lived in an international dorm at the University of Michigan, and one of the Indian guys down the hall had taught him a few curse words in Hindi, including one Marvin remembered to this day: *bhenchod*, which his friend had translated as "sister fucker," and which Marvin had for some reason found enduringly amusing, as he explained to a young lady from Baltimore as she sipped a cloudy drink from a martini glass. "A young lady"—his half sister! The context being, they'd both spotted the dogcatcher shamelessly hitting on the Asian studies professor. Though if he was forced to be completely honest, Marvin would've had to admit that his injection of sister-fucking into the conversation was not wholly innocent of suggestive intent.

She didn't bite, though. Or rather, she might have, but they were interrupted by another half brother, who introduced himself—this sort of interruption was happening all evening, of course, the "reunion" being a reunion of complete strangers, after all—and who turned out to be the only working musician Marvin would meet that evening. He lived in Nashville, he said, where he'd been doing steady session work as a bass player for the past decade or so. "Stuff you'd never have heard of, man," he told Marvin, chuckling, "unless you're into Garth Brooks." "You've played on Garth Brooks records?" Marvin asked. "No, that's just an example," his bass-playing half brother said. "Cats like him, though." Marvin nodded. He'd never had any real affinity for music; played no instruments, listened mostly to the radio in his car, or to one of a handful of the same albums he'd been spinning since college, best-of compilations by Al Green, the Police, Bob Marley, Prince. Some older rap. The newer stuff all sounded the same to him, knuckleheaded and abrasive, though he realized this probably just meant he was getting old.

They also couldn't help resenting the old man, as much as they found him intriguing, the mystery of him. His songs played on a loop, and whenever the most famous one came up, they joked about how Hawkins should've thought about casting a second spell that would have prevented his women from getting knocked up. Others wondered darkly if the spell in question, like so much magic, came with a curse attached, and if perhaps they were the result of that curse, the unintended consequence of Jay's version of the monkey's paw. *You can fuck all the women you want, but every single one of them's leaving pregnant . . .*

Seventy-five children, he'd apparently estimated before he kicked! The insane numbers had been reported in the papers as a "News of the Weird" type of story, though to many of them, it wasn't terribly funny but rather disquieting. Would anyone want to claim membership in such a messy diaspora? Not long after his mother's confession, Marvin locked himself in the bathroom and began vomiting into her doily-covered toilet. He'd always instinctively hated the man who'd screwed her and run off to the war or to the next gig—wherever he'd gone—partly because Marvin was a bit of a mama's boy himself. When he got older, he told friends he wished his mother would date, but in his heart, he clutched her love with greedy fingers, uneager to share. Now, finally having a face to put on her fleeting suitor—what a face!—it simply wasn't easy to stomach. *This guy?* he'd wanted to shout at her. Jesus, the man was a clown! And the music, such camp. He'd popped the disc from his car stereo after only a few listens, switching to the jazz station to cleanse his palate. The CD case would glint from the passenger seat floor for the next several months, mocking him.

Why had he come to the reunion, then? Well, curiosity, of course. That was the main thing. "And, well, I don't know." He was trying to explain himself to his Baltimore sister and country-bass brother. "As disgusted as I was, upon first learning of all of *this*—" He gestured at the crowd, quickly adding, "No offense. But it did mess with my sense of, I don't know. Uniqueness? But then I thought about it some more, and I realized, in a certain way, this made me, makes us, *more* unique. I mean, how many other people have a miniature army of siblings out in the world, biologically programmed to have one another's backs? That's the dream, at any rate. Except I'm still trying to get my head around the strength of the connec—"

He'd lost them. The Nashville brother had cocked his head in the direction of the ether, trying to make out the song that'd come up, and their sister was watching this professional appraisal play out on his face. Marvin hadn't heard the song before, either. It was a ballad, delivered with unusual sincerity, at least for their pops.

> My only prayer will be
> Some day you'll care for me

Marvin had to admit that, as the evening wore on, his father's music had begun to take on a certain power. The exceedingly strange context played a part, no doubt, along with his own increased inebriation. True, all true. But there was something in the repetition as well.

But it's oooooonly maaaaaake believe

The Nashville brother turned back to them and mentioned that he'd received a letter from a conceptual artist based in Berlin. The artist planned to remake all thirty-one Elvis Presley pictures, only with Screamin' Jay as the lead—well, "Screamin' Jay," an actor playing him, obviously—a response, the artist wrote, to Hawkins' claim that he'd been offered the script for *Jailhouse Rock* before Presley, only to be rejected by studio bosses as "too scary" and "too black." The artist had seen a photograph of the session player in a news story in *Der Spiegel* about Jay's children and found the resemblance uncanny, and she wanted to talk to him about being her Jay. The Nashville brother said he was considering the offer, though he'd done some research on her earlier work, which involved quite a bit of nudity along with certain Christian imagery that could be interpreted as sacrilegious, and worried it might prove controversial in a way that could hamper future gigs. "Nashville's still a pretty conservative town, you know," he said.

Marvin—really, all of them, to a half sibling—had nurtured secret hopes of the party turning into something like an actual family reunion. Not immediately, of course, but over the course of the evening, primed by booze and the power of suggestion and—who could say?—a certain sort of striving, a refusal to take no for an answer, born of the same stubborn Hawkins gene that, collectively, would bond the group in ways they could never predict. They wanted, in other words, to believe in the triumph of nature.

"Conway Twitty," the country session musician finally muttered.

They vowed, as they parted ways at the end of the night, to do it again each year, in different cities, to never lose touch with one another. But the cameras only came the one time, and it's not clear if they ever followed through.

CHAPTER NINE

Jailhouse Rock

You know, when they decided to make a *March of Time* newsreel about Lead Belly? The producers costumed him in prison stripes. The audience for colored folk music was limited. But as sung by a man who had killed another man, well. Call it P. T. Barnum, but more people paid attention. In real life, Lead Belly favored tailored suits.

Likewise, Hunk Houghton (Mickey Shaughnessy), a stocky hillbilly crooner who hoards packs of cigarettes in a foot locker, understands the appeal of a certain kind of authenticity. After they get out of the joint, he promises Jay Everett ("Screamin' Jay" Hawkins), his new cellmate, they'll partner up and embark on a concert tour.

We'd be a natural together!

Huddled in that cell, night after endless night, it was impossible not to feel like brothers. Little boys defying lights-out. As newbie, Jay got stuck with the top bunk. He didn't mind. Sometimes he'd reach up and spider-walk his fingers across the cracked ceiling. Even his hands pacing. If they talked, they had to whisper, or else risk attracting a screw, who would bang on the bars of their cage with a rousting stick or shine them with one of the blinding torches. Darkness was required to sell the stories they spun at one another, to shroud the harsh and distracting details of the unfabled world with mystery and allure.

Both ex-cons! The publicity would be sensational . . .

* * *

Or rather, not a spider. Something three-legged. His thumb and pinkie, wobbling with the movement of the middle fingers as if to provide balance, had otherwise devolved into vestigial uselessness. He watched his fingers scamper along the ceiling, his hand curled into the bird-shape of a spellcaster's, and considered the hoodoo it might yet pluck from the air.

Hunk, some nights, serenaded the rest of the cell block with plaintive songs about the passage of time. Days gone by, one step closer to the Lord, that sort of thing. Afterward, he'd take a little bow. Jay thought his playing up the irony made the gesture no less pathetic.

Hunk's the one who teaches Jay to play guitar. At first, Jay finds the lessons embarrassing. The only tune he knows all the way through happens to be a love song, its lyrics flattering a young girl on the subject of her beauty. Feels a bit off, delivering such sentiments to a convicted safecracker. Perhaps that's why Jay holds the instrument in such an unusual manner: with one hand, by the neck, hanging vertically, so that it looks like a duck he's just shot. He's distancing himself from the guitar, also making the act more obviously performative. The other hand, slow and methodical, plucks out the chords.

Jay never considered himself a singer before he got sent away. This was back in the days of the prison talent show, when the public still believed in reform. Even for someone like Jay, who had beaten another man to death in a bar fight!

* * *

Not that the penitentiary could be held up as a model of progressive advance. When Jay is punished by the cruel warden for his part in a mess hall riot, guards strip off his shirt and bind his wrists to a pipe running along the ceiling, his arms stretched behind his head in a position suggesting medieval torture. Then one of the screws, holding a whip, stands to the rear, while the warden counts off the lashes.

Jay tries to remain stoic, but as his face fills the screen, the audience tracks his tears.

Tough woodchuck, huh? the warden snarls.

At the start of the picture, Jay is working a construction job in a small town upstate. It's payday, and he decides to stop for a drink at a local tavern. Conversations fall quiet for a moment as he enters—he's the only black patron—until the bartender greets him effusively. Jay pulls out his check and asks if he can cash it. Then, in what's clearly become a friendly routine, he challenges the bartender to an arm-wrestling contest. Loser buys a round of drinks. When the bartender, a significantly older man, bends Jay's wrist to the counter with a minimal effort, cannier viewers will suspect Jay has thrown the match.

In prison, Jay is made to shovel coal alongside the other inmates. Here, too, he removes his shirt, and his face and torso become filthy with soot.

* * *

A woman eyes Jay conspicuously from the other end of the bar. Eventually, she sidles over to the stool beside him, asks if he'll buy her a drink. It's a strange request since he has just loudly announced his intention to purchase a round for the house. Still, Jay takes the bait. They're flirting when her husband arrives.

A fight breaks out.

We don't use hands here, the warden informs Jay upon his arrival. *We use guns.*

Back on the outside, Jay forces himself on his business partner and love interest, Peggy Van Alden (Judy Tyler). A rough kiss. Peggy's body language, the way in which she feebly resists, the very look in her eyes, implies, on some level, she might welcome the violation.

It's the beast in me! Jay snarls.

At his first meeting with Peggy, Jay allows his eyes to fall below the belt of her skirt, causing her to blush.

Peggy: *I'm glad you find me pleasing.*

Jay: *I don't find you nothin'!*

Jay crowds into the listening booth at the record store with Peggy. She places the recording of his song—"Don't Leave Me Now," his very first!—on the turntable and sets the needle in the groove, the blank sleeve of the 45 trembling in her hand because she already suspects what innocent Jay could never have guessed. Still, when the voice of Mickey Alba, another singer, drifts from the speakers, Peggy audibly gasps, and seems almost ready to swoon. Jay, for his part, can't grasp what he's hearing. How could Alba have stolen his song, his very arrangement?

Adding to his confusion is the excitement he feels, being in such close proximity to Peggy. This scene, we should note, takes place well before the first kiss. When Peggy leans into Jay, as if the edge of the spinning platter might slice her like a blade, his hand brushes the suprisingly rough material of her skirt and sends a charge up his arm. The air in the little booth begins to grow close. But he does not want to open the door, even as the stolen song continues to taunt him.

After Jay's career takes off, he performs on a television special. Because the song is about prison, they dress Jay like an inmate and have him dance in a set designed to look like a cellblock. One of the network censors is convinced the phrase *jailhouse rock* is prison slang for anal sex, but he is overruled by his colleagues. Jay secretly meant for the song to have a double meaning, though.

Inexplicably, the set also contains a fireman's pole.

The actress cast as Jay's love interest in the film within the film, Jay by this point having "made it" as a rock-and-roll star and subsequently "gone Hollywood," seems initially repulsed by her uncouth hick of a leading man. But when it comes time for their onscreen love scene, Jay grabs her with an unexpected brusqueness and steals a long and inappropriately passionate kiss. As with Peggy, his "real life" love interest, the actress finds herself titillated by this brutish gesture.

Possibly true story: Hawkins' claim that he punched Atlantic Records cofounder Jerry Wexler in the mouth during a recording session, after Wexler stopped a take for the fifth time.

Sing it just like Fats Domino, man, Wexler allegedly insisted.

He started up again, Hawkins would recall, *and then, POW!*

In the movie, Jay's character also resorts to violence when dealing with record label suits, bursting into the office of an unscrupulous executive and slapping him across the face.

Hunk balks at walking Jay's dogs. This is after Jay has become famous. Out of gratitude for giving him his start in music, Jay has kept Hunk in his employ, if grudgingly, and he derives especial pleasure in humiliating the older man.

It's not like I'm asking you to shine my shoes, Jay snaps after one of Hunk's complaints.

The story of Elvis saying the only thing niggers were good for was buying his records and shining his shoes is now widely considered apocryphal.

Later, Hunk punches Jay in the Adam's apple. Jay really did have it coming. But when his throat swells and he's rushed to the hospital and it looks as if he might never sing again—it's almost too much to bear! To have come this far, and then be derailed by a stray blow!

Of course, it was a punch, in a sense, that launched his career.

Jay! He's had enough!

Jay hesitated, his fist hovering. The jealous husband had slumped into the corner, a trickle of blood leaking from his mouth. Perhaps he had already begun to die.

A jazzy, instrumental version of "When the Saints Go Marching In" played on the jukebox.

Once, Hunk had been "swimming in gravy." This was before he'd gotten mixed up with a bad girl.

Does Jay loathe Peggy on some level, or love her? Or does he love only money? One night, they lie beside each other on his bed, discussing what Jay wants most in the world. He gazes into the distance, thinking only of his career and of the color of the car he might one day purchase.

Is that all you're interested in? Peggy asks.

Jay fails to pick up on the hint.

His first time in the studio, Jay does not immediately recognize the importance of finding a way to make each song his own. Instead, he attempts to imitate the style of other popular musicians. But it doesn't work; he sounds flat, unconvincing.

After the second take, though, even the jaded studio engineers nod their heads and tap their heels on the beat. So that truly is the secret. People want to hear something real, coming directly from you.

CHAPTER TEN

Gilchrist's Ghost

Billy had been the one who called Jay and invited him down to the gig. They were looking to replace Jimmy Gilchrist, the Fat Man's opening act and hype man, a blues shouter and notorious dope fiend, who had died in the snow outside the Douglass Hotel in Philadelphia two weeks prior.

The Fat Man, at that time, had the number one record in the country. It was 1954.

That first meeting took place in Newark, backstage after a show, the racket of a half-dozen conversations buzzing around the dressing room alongside music from a transistor radio: a bebop tune, probably Red Sultan's jazz show. The Fat Man took up the middle three-quarters of a couch, silently cooking a creole feast. A postshow ritual, Billy Diamond, his bass player and unofficial capo, had explained, having come about as a means of avoiding Jim Crow during swings through the South.

"Antoine's not about to go to the kitchen door of a restaurant and beg some Negro cook to sneak him out a plate," Billy said. "Hell no."

The Fat Man's real name was Antoine. In the dressing room, he had three burners going: your obligatory red beans and rice, a nice gumbo, and a batch of that Cajun gravy called roux. The rest of the coffee table had been crowded with unmarked jars of seasoning, a pitcher of sweet tea, a bottle of Scotch, some dried sausage on a cutting board, chopped bits of onion and okra and hot pepper that somehow missed the pot, and a half-eaten roast beef po'boy diagonally bisecting an issue of *Life* magazine. The crumbs from the sandwich gave the blond starlet on the cover a patchy five o'clock shadow.

"Antoine?" Billy said. "This is Jay Hawkins. The singer."

Jay, extending his hand. "Pleasure, Mr. D. I'm a great fan of your work."

The Fat Man peered up from the spoonful of roux he'd been cooling with his mouth and thrust out his free hand, his left, which, with an awkward, underhanded gesture, he grabbed Jay's right, giving it a loose pump.

"Yeah," he said, affecting a mild enthusiasm, the target of which, Jay or the slurped spoonful of roux, remaining unclear. The Fat Man held on to Jay's hand for several beats too long, a cheat means of rapidly conveying intimacy and comradeship, though his gaze had already shifted back down to the far-right hot plate, where the gumbo had started to bubble over. Shifting his spoon to a pencil's grip, he began to adjust the heat, making Jay feel like a mooring post, standing there stiffly at the far end of the business, while the Fat Man bobbed over the scent cloud of his hissing pots as if afloat. Eventually, the fingers of his left hand straightened, and the hand itself, like an expired trout, slid from Jay's grip.

"So I take it you've heard about our recent . . . job opening?" Billy said.

Jay nodded. "Tragic, man. Tragic."

Jay had caught Gilchrist's act about nine months earlier, up in New York. He glanced at Buddy Hagans, the sax player, who was preoccupied with an extremely young-looking girl, her false eyelashes visibly quivering with little mouthlike flutters from all the way across the room. Supposedly, Hagans had been the one trying to keep Gilchrist awake the night he passed, walking him around in that blizzard. Jay pictured him and the dying man in the shadows of that hotel, kicking up flashbulb-bursts of fresh snow. Gilchrist had been a head taller than Buddy, at least. Must have been like dancing with a rolled-up carpet. Rumor had them both going down, toppling into the snow like young lovers playing at something they'd seen at the movies.

"Jimmy was tough," the Fat Man muttered, scraping the sides of the gumbo pot with his spoon.

Jay wasn't sure if he meant the loss of Jimmy was tough, or if Jimmy was a tough bastard who nobody thought would ever die, despite the hard way he'd lived. Or if Jimmy was tough to babysit on a tour. The Fat Man's expression revealed little.

He continued, "This was almost ready to stick."

Jay looked at Billy, whose own face showed no emotion, though he did tighten his lips in a way that wrinkled his mustache.

Then Billy said, "So, we're looking for a new opening act."

They played Sunrise, Louisiana. Independence, Missouri. Sweetwater, Texas.

The Fat Man never did say much. That night, Jay hashed out the rest of the deal with Billy, who'd led him by the arm to a private corner of the dressing room to talk. The numbers had struck Jay as the modest side of fair.

The Fat Man's crowds liked Jay enough. He'd sing for about twenty minutes, accompanying himself on piano and sporting a royal purple suit, the cape and skull and bone through his nose not yet part of the act. Then the Clovers, a vocal group from DC, came out, the Fat Man backing them on piano before performing his own set.

Jay got along well with the Clovers. There were five of them, led by the tenor-baritone Hal Lucas. Onstage, their matching suits had slightly baggy sleeves and hung a bit long, in keeping with a fashion of the day; occasionally, the harmonizing trio of Lucas, Billy Mitchell, and Matt McQuater would take two steps back, in perfect unison, to allow Bill Harris, the guitarist, to move forward and bask in the spotlight, presenting a brief solo of his own. Hal Winley, the bass singer, always stood apart, at his own microphone. His dramatic entrances were timed for maximum impact, though his face remained that of a whisperer, someone muttering a warning under his breath. *Look out, cop's coming this way.* Winley smiled throughout the set, showing off the slight gap between his front teeth, in a way atypical of people in need of dental work, though possibly having such a deep and potentially intimidating voice had taught him, early on, to overemphasize his gentility.

Lucas had been the one who'd come up with the name of the group. For the luck of it, he always said, denying he'd ever been thinking how "clover" also happened to be slang for reefer cigarettes.

If they'd booked more than one night at a club, they slept at a boardinghouse. The Fat Man toured with a steamer trunk that opened up to reveal a full bar, complete with ice bucket, shaker, jigger-cup, martini glasses and tumblers, and simple but elegant coasters bearing his initials. The trunk and its contents were strictly off-limits to the backing band and the opening acts, even Billy, barring express invitation from the Fat Man himself.

One night in Myrtle Beach, a small group gathered in the Fat Man's room after the show. Eventually the Fat Man, who had been drinking Teacher's Scotch straight from the bottle, pulled out his pocket knife. Shooing off the girls who sat on the edge of his bed, he yanked back the thin comforter, the bedsheets, the mattress pad, one by one the layers piled in a collapsed pyramid. Each time he undid another strata of Mrs. Terryton's precisely tucked handiwork, his tugs became more violent. A man tearing at fabric while holding a knife automatically conjures images of a rapist, and it unsettled the party mood, despite the Fat Man's attempts to keep up a light patter. They were all pretty drunk or on the way there. Somehow they'd gotten onto the topic of straight jobs. One of the girls allowed her right arm to lean into Jay's left, distracting him. She wore very little.

The Fat Man's first job had been working at a mattress

factory, which was why he eventually stabbed poor Mrs. Terryton's bed.

"Oh man, Antoine, that's not nice."

The Fat Man said, "What? I didn't touch the sheets."

When the tip of the knife penetrated the skin of the mattress, it made a faint popping sound, followed by a deflating hiss, as the blade eased into the soft guts of the thing.

"Want to see what we all had to breathe in those days?" the Fat Man asked, adding, "Probably took a year off my life."

The workers at the factory had all developed hacking coughs from filling their lungs with the dust created by the various mattress stuffings. Even the Fat Man, whose main duty consisted of fastening fourteen-gauge coils to wooden box-spring frames, remembered visible clouds drifting in his direction, clear from the other side of the warehouse. He would try to work one-handed, he said, turning the washer with the same hand that held the stiff new spring steadily in place, while his other hand, the one that would normally be used for steadying, pressed his upturned shirt collar across his nose and mouth like Dracula's cape. Even then he was singing, and he certainly didn't want to be inhaling that shit.

Now he pulled the knife toward him, a hunter dressing a deer. As the fabric separated, it sounded like a tight zipper being roughly opened. Everyone instinctively took a step or two back from the bed once the Fat Man started working that knife like a lever, except for Walt "Papoose" Nelson, the guitar player in the Fat Man's band and the only person in the room still seated. The standing-room crowd made it impossible for Papoose to see what was going on, so he just grinned vacantly at all of the motion, flashing a gold tooth.

"Mattress factory, I knew I had to get out of that place.

My folks said, "'Tit Frère'—that's what they called me, 'Tit Frère—'why would you talk about quitting a solid job like that job you've got at the mattress factory? Don't you know people would kill for that gig?'" He pronounced it *teet,* not *tit.* "They had their way, I'd still be breathing that mess. Testing springs!"

Jay pictured the Fat Man on a factory floor, bouncing up and down on a spring, and did his best not to smile.

As the Fat Man spoke, he'd thrust a meaty forearm into the mattress, having first pushed back his shirt and jacket sleeves, and began rooting around like a country veterinarian delivering a cow. Jay, in the meantime, had slipped his own arm around his girl and begun to massage a point on her lower back, just above where things started to curve.

The Fat Man yanked out a fistful of stuffing. It looked like one of those tumors that you see in magazines, the kind that grow hair and teeth.

"So what have we got here? Horse's hair. A common stuffing. Scraps of old wool and other varieties of fabric. This is what they call 'flock' in the trade."

The Fat Man plucked an example of what he described from the clutched ball of stuffing, held it up for the crowd's examination, finally allowed it to flutter to the floor, like the petal of a rose.

Someone said, "Loves me not."

"Dried corn husks," the Fat Man said. "Cheap, also popular. Be careful, though. You use too much of this stuff? The padding could get prickly."

The handle of the pocket knife jutted from the mattress like the evidence of a crime.

*   *   *

One of the Fat Man's first hits had been "Junker's Blues," though he never messed around with the stuff. Nor did Jay. The surviving hopheads in the band, including the alto sax player Wendell Ducage, the drummer Cornelius "Tenoo" Coleman, and Papoose, had been forced to be more discreet after Gilchrist's death. Papoose, who had been known to pawn his instrument for drug money, generally handled the scoring of it. He had a smoky way of moving through a room, meaning he *drifted*, as if propelled by subtle forces not of his own volition, even the least significant gestures enacted with inexplicable cool. The way he squeezed little ice cubes from his fist into an empty tumbler, the shards dropping slow as turds. How his lighter's flame performed its own seductive dance for the trembling tip of a cigarette, the withholding of the touch approaching the erotic. Or even the lazy ease of his smile, the way his mouth kind of fell open, revealing a dull glint from that gold tooth, just a flicker, bringing to mind a stripper's slipped shoulder strap, the expert way it passed for accident, mere gravity. Sleepy eyes, sleepy limbs. Watching him move through the world, through a room, Jay couldn't help but read some extra presence in tasks that proceeded as reflex for other mortals. The fact that a greater speed would likely result in Papoose drooling, missing the glass entirely, or setting his tie on fire was beside the point. His pace of things didn't come off as a disability. It felt inherent.

As the tour progressed, Jay gained confidence as a performer. He'd been nervous, at first, unused to the fervid and youthful partisanship of the Fat Man's audiences. By El Paso, though, after closing with a Louis Jordan medley, he strode from the stage like an unrepentant killer. After watching the first couple of Clovers numbers, he slipped outside for some air.

It was a clear autumn evening, and the oceanic Texas sky threatened to send reeling any profligate gazers upon her astral majesty. Jay'd had a couple of tokes from Papoose's reefer cigarette before the show. The parking lot, full of cars, remained empty of people, save a quartet of white boys with glistening hairdos, all wearing leather jackets. The shortest one was performing some sort of trick with a knife, or else threatening to stab all of the others, it was unclear to Jay from his distance. One of the boys appeared to glance in Jay's direction but made no sign of recognizing him from the show. Perhaps they didn't have tickets. Jay considered sneaking them in the back door.

At this point, Jay noticed a presence in the shadows beside him.

"Evening, friend. Didn't see you there . . . Wait, have we met before?"

Stepping out of the gloom, a tall black man revealed himself. He wore a fashionably cut maroon suit, wingtips, a fedora, and a bright tie the color of fake blood, and he extended his hand in what appeared to be a greeting, but which turned into the opening movement of a theatrical swoop of the arm, ending with his palm cupped over his heart. *Look again!*, the gesture seemed to say. *You're* still *not sure if we've met?*

"Gilchrist?" Jay said.

"Call me Jimmy," said the ghost. "Or Gil. Some folks prefer that."

"But you're—"

As the words came out, he stopped, feeling as if he were reading a script.

"That's true," Gilchrist concurred. "And yet—here I stand. As you live and breathe."

"Is this a trick?" Jay asked. Except he'd seen a newspaper obituary after Gilchrist's death.

"Hey, man, it's baffling to me, too," Gilchrist said, lighting a cigarette. "Honestly, I never gave dying much thought, but if you had pressed me on the subject, prior to my firsthand experience, I would've probably told you I expected a long nap, minus the dreams and the waking up."

Jay opened and closed his eyes several times in an exaggerated, calisthenic fashion.

"You are not hallucinating," Gilchrist said.

"The problem here," Jay said, "is I don't believe in ghosts."

Gilchrist said, "You'll get no argument from me, pal. You're talking to a rationalist."

"Are you"—Jay almost choked on the word, out of a mixture of superstition and feeling absurd saying such things aloud—"*haunting* me?"

"Now why would I be haunting you? You see a sheet on my head? Feel some kind of tomblike chill?"

"I don't know. I took your place. Would be understandable, feeling peevish at a man's taking your place. Even though you're gone."

"Well, of course, I'd be lying if I said I felt no envy whatsoever. Would I love to be up on that stage, performing among the living? Certainly I would. But I don't blame you for my current state. Nor do I blame you for taking the opportunity when it called. Be like if you married my widow."

"You've got a widow?"

"Stay the fuck away from her. The widow's just an example. I'm just saying, there are no hard feelings. I only want the best for you. Well, okay, that's not true. I don't know you, and so don't really care either way how it goes for you, you want total honesty."

Jay nodded and shrugged. "That's fair, I suppose."

"So why am I here, then? I wish I could tell you. I just . . . *am*. Maybe you return to the spot where you departed, if you end up returning. *Spot* being a general term. In my case, meaning the people I was with."

"Right. But they haven't seen you yet?"

"Nah. Feel like it might be weird for them. Not that it's perfectly normal for you. I understand. But we weren't particularly well acquainted, so there's not that added emotional trauma of the return of someone you knew and if not loved at least tolerated."

Jay nodded again and said, "Makes sense." Then added, feeling like, since Gilchrist was the visitor, he needed to be hospitable, "What do you want to do?"

Gilchrist said he didn't know, that he hadn't given it much thought. Jay suggested going back inside and watching the rest of the show, but Gilchrist shook his head. He'd already seen it too many times to count.

"Papoose and them guys reform their ways?"

Jay said he was afraid they hadn't.

Gilchrist sighed. "Thing about dope is, it doesn't necessarily mess with your playing. Hard boozers are the ones who get sloppy, because they can't regulate their intake, not like junkies can. Whiskey, gin, another brand of whiskey, they'll all get you drunk in a different ways, and your musicianship will be affected accordingly."

Jay wasn't sure about all of that, but the talk of liquor made him thirsty. They ended up drinking tequila in a cantina in Juárez, just across the border. Gilchrist's ghost remained invisible to the rest of the breathing world, so Jay chose a corner bar stool and attempted to conduct his end of the conversation in low, muttery tones, his back to the other patrons, though with each subsequent cocktail his discretion flagged exponentially, until the shouting, gesticulating *gringo negro* had become a topic of much amusement.

Throughout the evening, Gilchrist kept him company by sipping from a silver flask that he'd produced from his jacket pocket. It seemed to be having an effect on Gilchrist's person: by the end of the night, his anecdotes became looser, his attitude more flamboyantly argumentative. Jay, in his own tipsy state, wondered if ghosts could even *get* drunk, if perhaps Gilchrist was merely reenacting his memories of inebriations past, in an effort to make Jay feel less self-conscious.

When it came to news from the afterlife, Gilchrist had little of use to impart, no glimpses of angels, heavenly Fathers, or even fellow spooks to report. Mostly, they talked about Gilchrist's past. Girls bird-dogged. Gigs nailed to the floor. His time touring with the Fat Man.

"You find him stuck up?" Gilchrist asked. "Everyone likes to say, 'Oh, the Fat Man just taciturn.'" He snorted, then related a long, mocking anecdote culminating in the Fat Man fanning himself with a stack of thousand-dollar bills pulled from his vest pocket.

Gilchrist waved his hand melodramatically while he

talked. When another customer grabbed for his stool, he made a big show of dodging the incoming body, stomach sucked in, arms assuming a stick-up position, all the while shouting with mock annoyance, "Whoa whoa whoa, partner. What's the rush?" The unseeing sitter, meanwhile, gave a neighborly nod as Jay switched positions to better converse with the ghost.

"So, I always thought the point of spooks was unfinished business," Jay murmured, sotto voce.

"Unfinished business? Well, *yeah.*"

Gilchrist leaned into his face. Minus the expected smell of shaved cheek or hot booze breath, the proximity felt surprisingly uninvasive.

"I never got to have a career, is the thing. Not a real career, any case. Not the one of which I'd always dreamed. Cut short! Who knows what I might've become? Now it's too late for me, I understand that. I fucked it all up. Pierced myself with holes, swapped out my blood with junk. But I've still got my ambitions. Those did not pass away with my mortal vessel. And so I've come back to pass them on to you, my successor."

Jay felt slightly dizzy from all the tequila, but he managed to arrange his mouth into a wiseacre smile of brotherhood. Gilchrist's ghost looked serious, though. Memphis Minnie played on the jukebox.

The dead man said, "I want to make you a star."

After that initial encounter, the tour moved to Galveston, and Gilchrist went missing for a few days, prompting Jay to ascribe the entire evening to alcoholic delirium. But the ghost would visit on three more occasions.

The first came after the final Texas show, en route to Louisiana. Jay typically rode with most of the Clovers in their station wagon, but this time, he wound up in the backseat of the Fat Man's sedan, Hal Lucas behind the wheel.

As Jay stuffed his duffel bag into the trunk, Gilchrist reappeared.

"Nice night for a drive."

Before Jay could respond, the Fat Man approached the car and handed him a two-gallon jar of pickled pigs' feet.

"You mind holding this in your lap, my man? I'm concerned I set it on the floor, there could be some sort of mishap. Hate to waste a drop."

Gilchrist grinned like a fool. Jay trying not to look.

"Not a problem, boss."

Gilchrist slid into the backseat next to Jay.

"Careful, now, you don't spill any of that precious brine."

Jay glanced up front, determined that both Lucas and the Fat Man had their eyes on the road, then flipped Gilchrist a jar-obscured bird.

"I'm just messing around, man. I'm dead! You going to stinge me these pathetic little pleasures?"

Gilchrist leaned over, so that he was inches from Jay's ear.

"I'm a teaser," he said. "My mother always said that about me. *Boy, why are you such a teaser? You leave your sisters alone, you hear me!* I can't help myself. It's my version of intimacy."

Jay, of course, could not respond.

Gilchrist went on, "The Clovers. I love how Hal comes up with the sweetest harmonic arrangements, but all of his songs are about drinking and fucking. *I got six extra children from gettin' frisky* . . . You should ask him about the first time they played the Apollo."

Jay, partly in hopes of shutting up the ghost, leaned forward and said, "Hal, you ever tell me about the first time you played the Apollo?"

Lucas glanced back, surprised by the question but also clearly pleased at the interest.

"You never heard the story of how Porto Rico chased us off the stage?"

"Who?"

"Stagehand at the time. A sort of mascot. Almost, picture one of them rodeo clowns."

"He wore a dress, was his thing," the Fat Man said.

"So that first night, we'd got about halfway through 'Blue Velvet' when that plantain-eating queen—"

"Anyone know if he even actually Puerto Rican?" the Fat Man asked.

"I heard he's a dark Italian," Gilchrist offered.

"That skirt-wearing sister—" Lucas continued.

"Didn't he like girls, though?" the Fat Man said. "I always thought the skirt was a bit. He liked to play peek-a-boo."

"So we're halfway through 'Blue Velvet,' and that nut-flashing pervert rushes onstage and starts firing off a *starter pistol*—"

Gilchrist chuckled. "I forgot the gun part."

"—yelling, 'Who let these amateurs on my stage? This ain't the Grand Ole Opry! This ain't a vaudeville stage in *Michigan*!'"

"Michigan," Gilchrist said, "meaning Peoria."

"We were pretty green. Pigmeat Markham followed us once. The first thing out of his mouth was, 'Fellows wearing suits that bad better either be selling me a Bible or not wanting to look too flashy for the judge.'"

"Pigmeat." The Fat Man chuckled.

"Show business." Gilchrist sighed. "That's what you'll find you miss most of all. The camaraderie. Us against the squares. You absolutely sure you're ready to leave the comforts of civilian life to join this tribe, kid?"

Jay mulled over the question while staring out the window of the Buick. By the time he turned back to face Gilchrist, the ghost had vanished.

Gilchrist's second reappearance came at the venue in Baton Rouge. Jay found the ghost seated on the piano bench when he walked onstage.

"Do you mind? Don't worry, I won't cramp your style."

Raising a hand to the smattering of applause that greeted his own appearance, Jay did his best to ignore the intrusion. The local authorities had decreed there would be two shows, the first white, the second black. Jay, looking out at the crowd, felt a twinge of self-consciousness.

"At least you're not the only brother on this stage, buddy," Gilchrist said. "You can thank me for that."

Jay slid onto the bench more aggressively than he would have, causing Gilchrist to scoot toward the edge.

"Hey! Watch it, now!"

Jay wondered what would happen if they touched. Would Gilchrist pass right through him, like in a book? Would he feel a chill in his guts?

Leaning into the microphone, he said, "Are you all ready to hear the Clovers?" The crowd roared an enthusiastic, nonverbal affirmation.

"Ofay bastards," Gilchrist said. "Not to state the obvious. But come on. What do they really want from us? Okay, you."

Jay began his set with a Wynonie Harris tune. He'd hoped the music would drown out Gilchrist's monologue, but the ghost had a supernatural way of projecting his voice.

"You just wait," Gilchrist went on. "Eventually, some peckerwood town will bar us completely from the white shows."

Jay watched as some of the kids nodded their heads.

During an instrumental passage, he shifted his gaze to his own hands, studying his fingers as they moved across the keys, as if he needed to, for concentration's sake.

" *'Sorry, boys, no colored allowed inside for this set. Y'all gonna have to wait your turn out here with the rest of yo' kind.'* You watch. They'll have us playing in the furnace room under the stage. Or in the parking lot out back. That fenced-in area where the garbage gets dumped? They can just pipe the music inside. And onstage, they'd have the cracker sheriff and his deputies pantomime the whole bit. Strumming on unplugged guitars, pounding at gutted-out pianos, moving their mouths to 'Your Cash Ain't Nothin' But Trash.' Can you see it?"

"*Look*, man, you can't do that anymore," Jay told Gilchrist in the dressing room after the show.

"Do what now?" the ghost asked.

The final appearance came at another venue, this time in Chicago.

When Jay arrived for the sound check, he discovered the Fat Man already present at the theater, pacing the stage. He'd just come from a ring-shopping binge, and his new acquisitions had put him in an unusually buoyant mood.

"How do you like my minnows?" he asked Jay, hands outstretched, palms down, his plump fingers erect and wiggling, all but the thumbs and right pinkie shackled in some form of decorative iron.

"What's the blue one?"

"Swiss topaz. The miners, way up there in the Alps? Each has his own St. Bernard dog with him. Instances of losing consciousness on account of oxygen deprivation are quite commonplace, you know."

"That doesn't sound right."

"Who's wearing the ring, me or you? Anyway, the point is not geology. The point is, you see that balcony up there?"

A lavishly gilded forefinger poked the start of an arc, leading Jay's gaze to the darkened, rearmost loft of the house.

"What I require of you, at the moment, is to climb up and let me know if the glint from my rings becomes in any way blinding or distracting while I'm playing."

"That's funny, man."

At this moment, Gilchrist stepped out of the wings. Actually, *stepped* is probably the wrong word. He performed more of a soft-shoe, confetti-scattering shuffle, mouthing the words *he ain't joking,* even though only Jay would have been able to hear anything had the ghost spoken aloud.

"I'm not joking. You think I only care about the folks up front, the ones I can see? Here's a valuable lesson you'd do well to heed: nobody gets to the top by ignoring the people in the back of the house. You want to make *them* happiest. Because if it works all the way back there, the love will come straight forward like a wave."

By the time Jay had made his way to the balcony steps, the Fat Man had already started into a tune, an old rag. Jay couldn't quite place the number. He refused to look at Gilchrist, who kept pace alongside him.

As soon as they entered the stairwell, Jay turned on the ghost and hissed, "You're a *figment*, man," pecking at his temple with his index finger for emphasis. "Nothing more than that. I've decided."

Turning on his heels, he continued up the stairs, but soon he felt the spectral presence leaning closer to his neck, followed by a soft exhalation—either that, or a draft. Then, in a ravaged, whispery baritone, Gilchrist began to sing.

> Figment Man
> Where's your pigment, man?
> You're all dream
> There's no seam
> Holdin' up those drawers!
>
> Figment Man
> I pulled a lig'ment, Sam
> Is that the way

I'll end my days?
Hobbled from chasin'
After too many plays?
And all the while
You'll keep on gettin' away
With (dig it, man)
Living un-im-pee-did-leeeee!
Why?
'Cause you dead, that's why!

And you're a figment, man!
(I wish I were a)
Figment Man!
(Why can't we all be)
Figments, mannnnnnnnn!

"I've heard worse," Jay had to admit.

By this point, they'd reached the balcony.

Jay shouted to the Fat Man that he was ready and waiting. The Fat Man stopped playing and yelled for lights. A toasty, off-yellow spot flickered on, trapping him and two-thirds of his piano in a honeyed sphere.

"Okay, *watch* me now," he called up to the balcony, before launching into "Blue Monday."

Gilchrist fired up a cigarette, took a thoughtful drag, and, upon exhaling, croaked, "Boss can still play."

The Fat Man arrived at an instrumental passage in the song. He took the opportunity to ask, "Am I blinding you?" He spoke in a louder fashion than he sang, and his voice boomed in the microphone.

Jay called back, "You're good."

To Gilchrist, he said, "No pianos in heaven, huh?"

Gilchrist chuckled. "Least of your worries, friend."

"You miss it, though? Performing?"

"I end up replaying moments in my head. My greatest hits. See the crowds' faces or my reconstruction of them. Who knows how much of what I think I'm remembering even really happened."

"I always hoped that all would be known. You know, on the other side."

"Hate to burst your bubble, kiddo, but despite what the living would like to believe? You know *less* on this side. It's all loss."

The Fat Man wrapped up the number and asked the lighting technician to switch filters. The spotlight turned a chillier white.

"I don't want to die," Jay said.

Gilchrist said, "You're a young man yet. Why worry now?"

Jay said, "So were you."

"Actuarially speaking, an anomaly. You know that. I wasn't living right."

"*Living right.* As if there's a way. People love to convince themselves they can beat the odds."

The Fat Man called out, "Are you *looking* or not?"

Jay said, "Sometimes I think it's the reason I do what I do. The reason I do *this*. It's not that you want to write songs that last forever. It's about wanting to make yourself so special, so alien a presence in the square world, you won't have to live or die by its rules."

The Fat Man cried, "I need some feedback down here!"

Darts of light flew from his fingers as they raced across the keys, a battery of miniature explosions.

The notion your specialness could merit exemption.

"Am I blinding you?" the Fat Man shouted. "You need to tell me if you're blind."

CHAPTER ELEVEN

Paris

Hawkins died six weeks into the new millennium, two days before Valentine's Day, at his home in Paris, from complications due to an aneurysm. He was seventy years old. He'd been living abroad with his sixth wife, Monique, a much younger Frenchwoman of African descent. Hawkins told an interviewer he'd picked her up hitchhiking one afternoon, that she'd just had her fingernails done.

None of Hawkins' obituaries noted the arrest that took place at the peak of his career. From the June 5, 1958, issue of *Jet* magazine:

> Rock 'n' roll singer Screamin' Jay Hawkins was questioned by Cleveland police after a 15-year-old girl, with marijuana among her effects, was found in his hotel room. The girl, described as a runaway from Akron, Ohio, was staying unregistered in Hawkins' hotel room, police said. The girl claimed the narcotics belonged to Hawkins, who had told her not to touch it. The singer was charged with failing to support his family in Cleveland.

That September, Hawkins, twenty-nine at the time and facing between three and thirty-five years in prison, pled guilty to possession of narcotics and statutory rape. Acccording to the music historian Bill Millar, Hawkins served a twenty-two-month prison sentence. Hawkins himself never publicly discussed his incarceration, or how white contemporaries who flaunted their own unsavory fondnesses for under-age girls somehow managed to avoid criminal charges. (A few months prior to Hawkins' arrest, Jerry Lee Lewis married his thirteen-year-old cousin, even though he had not yet divorced his first wife, who was fourteen; one year later, Elvis Presley began dating fourteen-year-old Priscilla Beaulieu while stationed at a German army base. Chuck Berry, on the other hand, was arrested in St. Louis in 1959 for transporting a fourteen-year-old across state lines. He served twenty months in prison.)

In the 2001 documentary *I Put a Spell on Me*, Hawkins does address the issue in an oblique way, telling the interviewer, "America wants to be able to control her blacks. If they can't control you, they will destroy you."

Then, mysteriously, and without elaboration, he continues, "They tried to destroy me on five occasions."

It's not clear what the other four occasions might have been. In a *Creem* profile, Nick Tosches writes that Hawkins "feels that there was some vaguely organized conspiracy that kept his records from getting airplay after 'I Put a Spell on You.' " During the same interview, Hawkins tells Tosches, "In those days, a nigger wasn't supposed to talk back, wasn't supposed to open his goddamn mouth. Wasn't even supposed to say the word nigger. Now things have changed 'cause they found out that some of those niggers will kill ya." In *I Put a Spell on Me*, Hawkins' friend Bo Diddley speculates that Hawkins may have left the United States because he could no longer abide the racism.

Long before he moved to France, Hawkins spent time in London in the mid–nineteen sixties. This came after his Hawaiian exile, where, supposedly, his girlfriend and singing partner, who performed as Shoutin' Pat Newborn, stabbed him with a butcher's knife after he took up with another woman. In Britain, though, he met with adoring crowds. "Stars and showbiz personalities rubbed shoulders with mods and even some rockers in Soho's Flamingo last week (3 February) to witness a fantastic display by Screamin' Jay Hawkins," went a 1965 article in the UK's *Record Mirror*. The writer described Hawkins as a "human tornado not seen in these parts for some time" and said that during the show, he knocked over amplifiers, had Henry smoking cigarettes onstage, and shot flames from his fingertips before playing the saxophone. Hawkins would remain in London for about two years, living at the White House, a hotel near Regent's Park.

Back in his home country, however, Hawkins struggled to find work or the appreciation he felt he deserved. When Tosches met him in 1972, the singer was forty-three years old and living with his second wife, Ginny, in a ninth-floor Broadway hotel room described by Tosches as "seedy." Tosches also took note of a ceramic, foot-shaped ashtray and an "obnoxious four-month-old Siamese cat named Cookie." When Tosches arrived, Hawkins, wearing horn-rimmed glasses, a Hawaiian shirt, and a knit cap, was in the middle of using a cassette recorder to tape a Frank Sinatra album (which was spinning on a record player); later, he played Tosches a new ballad called "Game of Love," about (Tosches' words) "some guy caught between his wife and fresh cunt." The playing of the tune angered Ginny, who disliked the way Hawkins sang about loving a particular woman forever. Despite his protestations, Ginny remained convinced that he'd written the line about some fresher stuff.

Hawkins complained bitterly about Dick Clark's refusal to play his music decades earlier, insisting his act had been ripped off by everyone from Melvin Van Peebles to Little Richard to the makers of the blaxploitation horror film *Blacula*. "Everybody at one time or another has taken a little something from me," he said, "and I get this impression that everybody's going places with what I was doing fifteen goddamn years ago. Everybody except me."

"Game of Love" did not become the hit record Hawkins hoped would resuscitate his career. Nor had "Constipation Blues," released three years earlier, though the album had merited a review in *Rolling Stone*, where the critic John Morthland claimed Hawkins "practiced black magic and headshrinking in the jungles of Haiti, and in the Orient, a chick who sung with him on a single called 'Ashes' tried to kill him with a knife." Morthland was less taken with Hawkins' delivery, pointing out that his baritone "has almost no range" and that he delivers "love ballads with almost the same phrasing and emphasis as in his monster songs. A crooner he is not."

In 1979, Keith Richards joined Hawkins in the studio to play on the inauspiciously titled number "Armpit No. 6." The pair also recorded an updated version of "I Put a Spell on You," which sounds funny today with its Rolling Stones guitar licks and disco-era production. Despite Richards' star power, both songs went nowhere.

The following year, Hawkins opened for the Stones at Madison Square Garden, after James Brown canceled at the last moment. By all accounts, Hawkins perplexed the young crowd, though they seemed to enjoy "I Put a Spell on You," which they recognized as a Creedence Clearwater Revival song. By the time Mick Jagger bounded onstage in flamboyant yellow pants, Hawkins had already left the arena, and he managed to make it home in time to watch that evening's wrestling match on television.

Hawkins was fifty-five years old. Not long after the concert, the writer Gerri Hirshey interviewed him at his Manhattan apartment. Still a "tall, robust man with square shoulders and a long, tensile reach," Hawkins spent much of the interview halving blood pressure pills with a hunting knife.

"Kiss was in diapers," Hirshey wrote, "when Screamin' Jay Hawkins pumped the full clip of a military automatic rifle into a wild boar on the rim of a Hawaiian volcano to extract the tusk that now thumps against his chest on a big gold chain."

There was a plastic Buddha on his coffee table, a library of books about voodoo and the occult, a blood-transfusion bottle hanging over the bar, a pile of old scrapbooks, and ledgers containing meticulous records of every gig.

"Now aren't you terrified," Hawkins asked Hirshey, "to be in the wild cannibal's den?"

At some point in the nineteen eighties, Rudi Protrudi, the lead singer of New York garage-punk band the Fuzztones, met Hawkins at a beer-and-ribs joint near St. Mark's Place. Hawkins had landed a steady gig there, just him and a piano, playing oldies by Fats Domino and Little Richard, none of his own material. The yuppie crowd talked throughout his sets, and the owner harassed him, telling him when to start and stop. Protrudi began chatting with Hawkins after the show, and he returned the following night, and the night after that, finally working up the courage to tell the singer that he had a band of his own, that he was signed to a small record label. Maybe, he offered, he could figure out a way to help Hawkins' career?

Hawkins replied, "I don't like white people."

Around that time, though, another white guy, the director Jim Jarmusch, made prominent use of "I Put a Spell on You" in *Stranger Than Paradise*. Throughout the film, Eva (Eszter Balint), a sixteen-year-old Hungarian visiting her cousin Willie (John Lurie) in New York, plays the song on a portable cassette player.

> WILLIE (*abruptly stopping the tape*): What the fuck is that?
>
> EVA: It's Screamin' Jay Hawkins, and he's a wild man, so bug off.

Hundreds of versions of "Spell" have been recorded over the years, but it's not entirely clear if Hawkins retained control of his publishing. His *New York Times* obituary claimed he had, and that unlike a number of African American artists of his era, he received royalties throughout his life. But according to Jarmusch, by the time of *Stranger Than Paradise*, Hawkins had sold off the rights to his best-known song, forcing the director to license it from a third party. Jarmusch still felt a personal need to pay Hawkins something, though, even though he had no legal obligation. He finally tracked down the singer in a New Jersey trailer park. Hawkins didn't even have a phone at the time, and he was surprised by the visit. For years afterward, whenever they ran into one another, Hawkins would insist, "I still owe you that money," no matter how often Jarmusch retorted, "But it wasn't a loan!"

Later, Jarmusch cast Hawkins as a Memphis hotel desk clerk in *Mystery Train*. Hawkins liked to mess with people on the set, but if you teased him back, Jarmusch said, his feelings easily bruised.

One day, when shooting was delayed because of rain, Hawkins took out a pouch of bones and began worrying them with his fingers. Then he told Jarmusch, "Okay, you can set up the cameras again—it's going to stop raining in five minutes." Jarmusch chuckled at the performance. But five minutes later the rain had stopped.

His personal life remained complicated. In *I Put a Spell on Me*, Hawkins lists his many wives. His first, he says, was a black girl from America; his second, a Filipino girl from the Philippines; the third, a black girl from Guadeloupe; the fourth, a Japanese girl from Tokyo. He's about to proceed to the last when an off-screen voice reminds him of a French girl. He laughs, surprised. He has forgotten a wife!

Deborah Roe, one of Hawkins' many children, told the *New York Times Magazine* she never even heard her father's name until she was twenty-three, when a cousin asked, "You know who you look like? You never heard of a man named Screamin' Jay Hawkins?"

"No," Roe said. "Who the heck is that?"

After confronting her mother, Roe drank an entire bottle of Johnnie Walker Red. Then she obtained Hawkins' phone number through an aunt. He was living in New York at the time, working nightclubs, and he agreed to meet her at the Port Authority Bus Terminal. "He did most of the talking," Roe recalled. "He told me that he used to get a shot from my mother in the phone booth on his breaks while he was entertaining in Atlantic City."

The interviewer didn't understand, so Roe explained: "Sex. From my mother in a phone booth on his breaks in Atlantic City. So I guess that's how I got here."

Another daughter, Sookie Hawkins, the product of an early marriage in Cleveland, said her father abandoned the family when she was in kindergarten; after a point, she stopped asking where he'd gone, because the question always made her mother cry. Sookie said she could count the number of his visits on a single hand. Once, he showed up driving a pink Cadillac and made the kids wash the car. Then he bought them popsicles. "And then he talked to me and told me that he loved me," she remembered. "And then he left."

Still, she listened to his music constantly, just to hear his voice, in hopes of acquiring some notion of what kind of man he was.

The last time they met, she surprised him at a club called Peabody's Down Under in Cleveland. Hawkins hadn't told his daughters he would be playing their hometown; Sookie just happened to notice an ad for the show in the newspaper. She and her sister went to the venue, where they were the only African Americans in the audience. Afterward, they pushed their way backstage and Sookie took the occasion to furiously berate her estranged father, releasing all of the pent-up feelings she'd held inside for so many years. "He just stared at me," she later recalled.

After the encounter, Hawkins remained in contact with Sookie's sister, but he refused to speak to Sookie ever again.

* * *

A Greek documentary filmmaker began following Hawkins in the months before his death. The singer appears older but not frail, his face unlined, his voice, whether performing or recounting another wild tale, still resonant. He has grown a thin Vincent Price mustache and often wears oversized granny glasses and a fuzzy beret.

"Here it is, 1999," Hawkins says at one point. "Almost *deux mille*."

Later, he tells the camera, "Well, I am still alive, and that's important to me. My next birthday I'll be seventy-one. Shit, I'm too damn old to get a hard-on. And I've got a hard-on!"

Joking aside, one notices how he gasps for breath while making his way up the hill to the Parthenon. Steps, the singer admits, have become hard for him.

He boasts to the filmmakers that he once told Paul Anka, "You'll die before me if I have to pay for it." He also tells them, "They took Sammy Davis' eye because he was making love to Kim Novak." And he claims that, in the nineteen fifties, a girlfriend begged him to take her to see the hottest musical act of the day, Elvis Presley. Hawkins says he managed to get them backstage, where he told Presley, "I don't know who you are, but my woman finds you amazing. I don't."

Shrugging into the camera, he adds, "Had to be honest with him."

The documentary revolves around a performance filmed at the end of 1999, at an opera house in Athens. For the concert, Hawkins wore a long, flowing wig. If not for his purple frock coat and cravat, the hair could almost pass for that of a heavy-metal singer's from the mid–nineteen eighties. But seated at a piano in such a costume, Hawkins makes you think of Mozart, or, rather, of Tom Hulce's portrayal of Mozart in the movie *Amadeus*.

Hawkins tells the crowd he can't wait to come back to Greece to begin making new records. But the concert would be his last. He never returned.

In 1980, he told Hirshey, "I wish I could be who I was before I was me."

Paradise, Hawaiian Style

He settled in Hawaii after getting out of prison, broke and largely forgotten. "I Put a Spell on You" had never generated significant royalties, so many radio stations having banned the record because of its "cannibalistic" moanings. The coffin stirred up even more controversy, and in the end, they cut Jay's performance from Alan Freed's early teeny-bopper picture, *Mr. Rock and Roll.* By the time of his release from the joint, more than a few adults had already written the obituary of the genre they'd always figured nothing more than a fad, the major players from the first wave of rock acts either dead or drafted or felled by disgrace.

Jay had originally considered the gig at Forbidden City a resting point, Waikiki a pleasant enough shore to find one-self beached. He would enjoy the weather, the live nude girls, while plotting . . . Well. Firming up specifics got hinky. He'd been at the club two years now, just him, sitting at the piano. Full costume, of course, with Henry by his side, but no box, no pyrotechnics, and not much in the way of original material. The crowd, comprised predominantly of gentlemen of a certain age, responded most appreciatively to bawdier jump blues numbers, rock and roll, in this setting, coming off as far too *innocent.* Better to dust off something by Lowell Fulson, Peppermint Harris, Eddie "Cleanhead" Vinson, maybe toss in a dirty joke for stage patter.

Girls rotated through the club with regularity. For the newcomers, Jay remained an object of curiosity. Surely he had to be more of a catch than the morbidly obese Hawaiian goons who worked the door, or the owner's speed-freak son Swanson. But Jay turned out to be a drunk who rarely spoke offstage, lived in a flophouse, and shuffled around town freaking out the children of Japanese tourists with his stupid outfit, oblivious and quite often muttering to himself. Rumors also circulated. According to one, his demand for record royalties had gotten him placed on some kind of mafia hit list; another had a quartet of exes combing the continental United States for him, the fourth the mother of the second. That's what they'd heard, anyway.

April, one of the new dancers, noticed the emcee always slipped out the stage door between numbers, which she found intriguing. She'd worked clubs in the Bay Area before crossing the Pacific, and in her experience, male hosts rarely missed the chance to linger and flirt, no matter how crowded the dressing room. One night, she decided to follow Jay outside. He gave her a look, sort of nodding without saying hello. April fought the urge to smile in return, instead simply raising her eyebrows in a languid manner suggestive, she hoped, of a mellow tropical cynicism, the consistency of the weather having somehow lowered the stakes.

They stood there smoking for a while. Eventually, Jay asked where she'd come from. "Welcome to paradise," he muttered afterward, in a tone April couldn't quite read as fully sarcastic. A group of drunk tourists wandered by, one of the men pointing at Jay, whispering something. The club stood on the far edge of a fairly well-trafficked street bordering Chinatown.

Certain of the other dancers pretended to find Jay's costume creepy, but April recognized a racial component in their mock disgust. She also couldn't believe she was the only one who remembered his original act. She'd been fifteen when her parents had dropped her and her older sister at the Moondog's Coronation Ball in downtown Philly. Jerry Lee Lewis, the Everly Brothers, the Cadillacs, and Fats Domino had all been on the bill, but Screamin' Jay Hawkins, busting out of his coffin, had made the strongest impression. She'd wanted so badly to say something the moment she laid eyes upon him at Forbidden City, but wasn't sure if it would make him feel old or too much like a has-been. Not saying anything, however, seemed such a miserly deprivation.

After the club closed, around four in the morning, Jay would have breakfast at an all-night chop suey joint: couple of fried eggs, easy-over and smothered with hot sauce, with a scoop of rice on the side. One morning, April followed him to the diner. Folding her legs beneath the counter two stools down, she ordered a coffee. Jay, lowering a newspaper still warm from the presses, gave her another look. She'd changed into street clothes: clamdiggers, a loose fuchsia blouse, and a light gingham shawl, the rest of her stuff hanging out of an oversized purse. Jay still wore his ghoul suit. April placed her bag beside Jay's staff, which leaned against the countertop, Henry eyeing her vacantly.

"Any new King sightings?" April asked. She meant Elvis Presley, who had returned to the island to film his latest movie, his second Hawaiian picture in as many years. The papers covered his every move, especially after he'd been spotted cavorting with his costar, Stella Stevens.

Jay snorted, his face displaying the first traces of emotion April had seen, aside from the exaggerated, theatrical contortions required for his act.

"*King*," he muttered, not looking up from the article he'd been reading. "Of what? Brylcreemed sissies?"

He smiled now, only slightly. "You know," he went on, "that hillbilly can't even swim?"

April knew for a fact Presley *could* swim, having just spotted him the other day at the pool of the Waikiki Hilton. But she didn't want to contradict Jay or sound like a gawking rube. Jay proceeded to tell a story about how he'd had to rescue Presley from drowning during the filming of *Blue Hawaii*. Hadn't been for yours truly, Jay said, one million Elvis fans would not only be afflicted with unaccountably bad taste but also shit out of luck when it came to any more terrible movies starring their greasy idol.

April saw her opening to bring up the Philly show. Instead, she blurted out, "Are you working on new material?" A foolish question! Was she conducting a fan club interview?

Jay frowned. "Oh yeah, honey, every night. I'm fixing to do an all-instrumental record of striptease piano rolls. This gig"—he jabbed a thumb back in the direction of the Forbidden City—"nothing but warm-up."

Then Jay told the story of the first time he met Presley, a few weeks prior to the near drowning. He'd been at the club, perfunctorily belting out an old Louis Jordan tune, when he noticed a commotion at the back of the room. It turned out to be Presley and a couple of his boys. Jay felt unnerved. He assumed they'd come for the dancers, though wasn't sure why they'd chosen this dump over any number of the more upscale spots in town. "No offense," he told April. He said he figured the choice of venues must have had to do with issues of anonymity.

After wrapping up the number, Jay made a couple of jokes, introduced the next dancer, and slipped backstage.

He'd been about to step outside for his customary tipple when Swanson pulled him aside.

"Someone who wants to see you," he said, gesturing to his own office, typically off-limits to all but whichever dancer currently happened to be in his favor.

Inside, Presley sat behind the desk, flipping through a fishing magazine.

"Mr. Hawkins," he said, smiling that smile of his. "Thank you so much for taking a few minutes to chat with me. Please, sit down." Jay, glancing back, realized Swanson had discreetly closed the door without following him inside, Presley acting like it was his own office now.

Thoughts ran through Jay's mind as he lowered himself into the chair, vague hopes too wild to seriously entertain. Weren't they? Could Presley possibly have come to snatch him out of exile, perhaps by casting him in a small but key role in the Hawaii picture? Might he need a song for the soundtrack, something easily played on a ukulele?

It turned out Elvis merely wanted to discuss the occult. Presley had a mystical bent, and when he'd heard Hawkins was performing on the island, he recalled talk about Jay's supposed investigations into the dark arts. He wanted to know if the stories could be true, and if so, would Jay be willing to share his secrets?

"What did you tell him?" April asked, perched now on the edge of her stool.

Jay's eyes flicked down to her cleavage. "Now that's a much longer story," he said. "Care to go for a stroll? The beach is rather pretty this time of morning."

They stepped outside, into the mazelike back alleys of

Hell's Half Acre, the notorious Honolulu ghetto, where tenements with wooden fire escapes and covered catwalks stood so close you could jump from one to the next in a pinch. As they passed beneath the tangle of laundry lines connecting the buildings, Jay pointed out a flipped-over tub the Chinamen used as a warning gong whenever cops showed up for a raid.

Elvis had been curious about black magic, in particular anything hinting at notions of personal immortality. "I've had a heavy death trip going," he told Jay. None of the trappings of fame seemed powerful enough to shake it.

Jay told Presley how Haitians guarded over freshly buried dead relatives, taking turns sitting up all night with guns and machetes, an armed shiva that could last for several weeks, until the body began to rot, by which point it would be too late for a grave robber to steal and zombify the corpse. Elvis dug this story. He wondered what Jay thought about the zombie state of mind. Like, if it could remember its life before dying? "Or do you suppose we're essentially dealing with soulless walking manikins, here?" Jay acknowledged that he couldn't say for sure, which seemed to displease Presley. Then Jay recounted another zombie story he'd heard, this one centered around a mysterious couple who turned up at a Haitian sugar plantation. This was back in the 1940s. The couple told the boss they could offer him extraordinarily hard workers willing to harvest cane for half of the going pay.

Their claims proved unexaggerated. The new workers toiled without complaint, never demanding extra breaks or water; as far as the boss could tell, they rarely even spoke. Of course, the men were zombies, slaving under the control of the wicked couple. Their reaping of the profits would have proceeded as envisioned, had not the husband's sister fallen ill. Summoned to her bedside on the opposite side of the island, the husband, before departing, warned his wife to keep close watch over their zombies. "It's especially important," he reminded her, "for the creatures to maintain a strict diet, for when a zombie tastes salt, it realizes it is dead."

After a few days alone, though, the wife grew bored. When she heard about a parade in town, she could not resist attending. Despite her husband's entreaties, she brought their zombie slaves along, in part because she worried about leaving them alone at the bunkhouse, but also, sentimentally, in hopes they might enjoy the outing.

Indeed, the parade was wonderful. The wife, her spirits raised, impulsively decided to buy the zombies a treat from a vendor selling sweet *tablette* cakes. She did not realize the baker had salted the pistachios before mixing them into the cake.

When the zombies tasted the salt, they emitted awful, inhuman screams. The wife collapsed in a faint.

After, the undead men marched back to their home village. Upon their arrival, widows, orphans, and bereaving mothers rushed from their homes, wailing in recognition of lost family members, believing a miracle had occurred. But the corpses remained insensate, their eyes betraying no recognition even as wives and children fell at their feet. Shambling on, the zombies refused to halt until they reached their own graves. There, touching the earth where they'd once laid buried, the bodies crumbled to dust.

Elvis grimaced. "What happened to that couple?"

After the villagers pieced everything together, Jay said, one of them stole a shirt from the husband and made an *ouanga* doll, stuffing it with goat's dung and piercing it with needles and cock's feathers dipped in blood.

Then, to be on the safe side, they hired some men to wait outside the husband's cabin and chopped his head off with machetes.

By this point, April and Jay had reached the edge of the beach. Kicking off their shoes, they stepped onto the cool sand, the tide gently breaking in the pink dawn. A handful of surfers had already begun hurtling themselves into the waves. They sat on one of the benches in front of Tubby Otis' fish and poi shack, not yet open for business. Inside, a group of men smoked furiously and seemed to be playing dominos for money. The beach curved parenthetically around the bay, and a morning fog hovered over the distant mountains, the Hawaiian slack-guitar music drifting from a transistor radio inside Tubby's perfectly framing the scene.

"So what happened with Elvis?" April wanted to know.

Presley, Jay said, continued pushing him on the voodoo thing, until finally he broke down and told him another story, this one personal, revolving around a ritual he once attended.

And then Jay began telling April the same story. The ritual took place in New Orleans, he explained. He could still remember passing over Lake Pontchartrain on that endless bridge, the water scooping up the moonlight like a big mirror, bathing their journey in an eerie glow. He rode in the passenger seat of a Buick, and when the car reached land again, it immediately plunged into a tunnel of cypress and haunted swamp, a muffled darkness oppressing the narrow road, only the quavery headlamps pushing it aside in endless, hysterical flashes, one curtain whisked away to reveal another, and another, on and on, Hawkins, meanwhile, staring at the driver's throat, where a scar almost perfectly traced a fat *accent grave* above his Adam's apple. Jay wondered, *Who gets themselves stabbed in the throat?* It had been hastily stitched, you could tell just by looking: a white streak of foam against the driver's dark skin, its edges smeared. Hawkins thought of a snail flattened by a tire. Also of the narrowly missed jugular. The cold, flat side of the knife threatening to twirl it like a fat noodle.

The knotted bundle at Jay's feet had squirmed. He reached down to still it. The cat throbbed like a muscle under the skin of the sack. Jay closed his eyes and sank into the passenger's seat, which hammocked his body in a yanked-up-from-below sort of way, at once precarious and tensile. After a few moments, he felt something light pass across his chest, then a pillow of humid air buffeted his face. The driver had reached over and rolled down his window. *We nearly there,* he muttered.

How they had parked and followed a path lined with marsh grass. How the air felt swollen and reeked with a pungent, swampy odor, raked leaves soaked in vinegar. How Jay held the sack away from his body, as if its contents might be the source of the stink, a soiled diaper. The cat, thrashing around inside, dispelled that illusion. Eventually, they reached a half-dozen men sitting around a fire, beating on drums with palms and tom-toms, shaking rainsticks and maracas, the calluses on their drumming hands glinting like jewelry in the firelight. A priestess, also working a set of maracas, seemed intent on repeatedly striking the same spot in the air, as if she were hammering an invisible nail. The driver touched Jay in the portion of his back between his shoulder blades, his spindly fingers surprisingly firm. Jay could feel the older man's uncut nails, their sharpness forming the base of the steeple. It was the part of his back where an archer might hope to empty his quiver.

Go to her, he said.

Hawkins began to move in the direction of the priestess. As she swayed to the drumming, she incorporated a head-bob into her motion that could be read as encouragement. The spectators who were not playing musical instruments had all fixed their gazes upon Jay. He glanced at one of the drummers, an obese man wearing a white, sheetlike smock over khaki pants and sandals, and gave him the fellow musician's universal nod of approval. The drummer remained stone-faced. There might be a prohibition on smiling at the initiate at this point in the ritual, Hawkins thought. He wasn't offended.

The priestess mouthed something, pointing at the ground. Like a sad tumbleweed, the sackbound cat, which Hawkins had set down, was attempting a blind, lumpy crawl out of the circle, instinctively moving away from the noise and the heat. Jay snatched it up. This action had an agitating effect. A flurry of Houdini-style contortions erupted from inside the bag. The priestess gestured toward the boiling kettle.

"Are you gonna tell me," Elvis said, "you boiled a live cat?"

Jay shrugged and decided to skip ahead to where the priestess and her helpers poured the contents of the kettle onto a circular patch of earth, about twice the size of an outhouse hole, the water releasing its trapped steam and causing the soil to darken and bubble. A heap of meat and skin and bones came into focus as the vapors thinned and dispersed, a reveal in the style of a flashback sequence from a Hollywood melodrama, only here not the heroine's first love, nor the hero's childhood wagon, but the loose and soggy parts of a carcass, which, after some squinting, emerged as clearly feline, one of the tented ears the giveaway, the priestess quickly disturbing the pile, spreading the remains around with the base of her rainstick, her eyes alert, scanning the offal as if it might contain a swallowed pearl, the cat's skin torn like fabric scraps on a dressmaker's floor.

Without looking up, the priestess told Jay, *Now is time for you to find the bitter bone.*

Elvis looked as if he might be sick. He asked Jay to get to the part where he gained powers or at least some mystical insight.

April, at this point, interrupted. "You never met Elvis. And you're not some voodoo priest. You're a washed-up singer in a costume." She was smirking, though, her accusations more teasing than hostile.

"Oh, so you don't believe me?"

"No. I don't believe you."

"You think I'm making all of this up?"

April couldn't read Jay's deadpan, but decided to press forward.

"I think you haven't spoken an honest word in so long, you've forgotten how."

"Tough crowd. Tough lady."

"Who said I'm a lady?" Giving him an opening, which he declined to take.

"Tell you what," he said, instead. "How about I prove it?"

"You want to find a pay phone, call up your buddy Elvis?"

"Not that. I don't have his number anyway."

"Convenient."

"What I could do, though, is show you some real voodoo."

"What, like a spell?"

"I wouldn't use that word, but sure."

"You're going to put one on me?"

"Again, that's not exactly how I'd have phrased it. But in essence, yes. Want to see it?"

"What exactly will I see?"

"Just say yes, and you'll find out."

"All right."

"All right yes?"

"All right yes."

April closed her eyes when he asked her to, flinching when she heard him take a breath and blow something into her face. A pinch of sand, most likely, at least that's what it felt like. Then he said, "Okay, you're good to look again."

She opened her eyes, half expecting to be greeted by Jay's leering face, or perhaps to find herself staring into the gaping eye sockets of that skull he carried around. But instead, he'd pulled back and assumed a sober mien, his head cocked expectantly in a way that made her giggle.

"I don't feel any different," she confessed.

"Oh, but you will. Just give it some time."

"How much time, exactly?"

"Couple of hours. Couple of days. Hard to say with any precision."

"And you won't say what I should expect to happen to me."

"It's better if you're surprised."

"But it might involve my falling in love with you, madly, obsessively, uncontrollably?"

"I can't rule anything out."

April said, "Well, I suppose that makes it more exciting!" Then she glanced at her watch. "Oh, shoot. I'd better run."

If Jay was disappointed, his face betrayed nothing.

"A prior engagement," April explained, dusting off the seat of her pants as she stood and gathered her handbag. "Sort of work related. I can't really say more. But I promised to meet a gentleman across town, and I shouldn't be late."

Jay nodded. As they said their good-byes, he offered her a swig from his flask, which she politely declined, saying she'd take a rain check, that she couldn't wait to experience the effects of whatever he'd just done to her, and that she'd be back to complain if it wasn't memorable, at the very least.

After the girl's departure, Jay moved from the bench onto the sand, closer to the surf, and sat cross-legged upon his cape, spread beneath him like a blanket. Looking over his shoulder, he watched as April paused at the grass and slipped on her shoes, giving him a final coquettish wave. Then he turned to face the ocean. Closing his eyes, he settled into the sound of the crashing waves and the occasional, distant cry of a gull. Passersby might have taken him for a meditative sort. But he was merely enjoying the feeling of the sea breeze on his exposed skin.

It had been a good line, he thought. The power of suggestion. Ages since he'd felt such stirrings. And whatever happened in the coming hours or days, it would be all his fault. Good, bad, uncanny, banal: *something* would occur to give her pause. His spell was cast. He had her now.

Selected Bibliography

Gerri Hirshey, *Nowhere to Run: The Story of Soul Music*; Nick Tosches, *The Nick Tosches Reader*; Scott Cohen, "Living Poets Society," *Spin* (April 1990); Karen Schoemer, "Screamin' Jay Hawkins as Pitchman and Actor," *New York Times* (April 5, 1991); Alix Spiegel, "Papa Was a Rolling Stone," *New York Times Magazine* (January 7, 2001); Albert Murray, *Stomping the Blues*; Stanley Dance, *The World of Swing*; Bill Millar, liner notes to *Spellbound* (Bear Family Records, 1990).

The joke about the monk, the devil, and the rooster comes from Arturo Graf's *The Story of the Devil*. Jay's story about the zombie-sharecropping couple in Haiti is adapted from William Seabrook's *The Magic Island*. The story of the voodoo ritual involving the cat and the bitter bone comes from Zora Neale Hurston's *Tell My Horse: Voodoo and Life in Haiti and Jamaica*. I first came across the Ernest Ansermet quote in LeRoi Jones' *Blues People: Negro Music in White America*.

Acknowledgments

Many thanks to my brilliant editor, Riva Hocherman, and my peerless agent, Jim Rutman; my generous early readers Manuel Gonzales, Julia Holmes, and Jessica Lamb-Shapiro; my editors at *Rolling Stone*, in particular Will Dana, Jason Fine, Jann S. Wenner, and Sean Woods; and my remarkably supportive family and friends, especially Italo and Anita Binelli, Paul and Julia Binelli, Jonathan Hickman, Eric Lindvall, Bill McIntyre, Dinaw Mengestu, and Jonathan Ringen.

MARK BINELLI is the author of *Detroit City Is the Place to Be* and the novel *Sacco and Vanzetti Must Die!* as well as a contributing editor at *Rolling Stone*. Born and raised in the Detroit area, he lives in New York City.